SPEAK
TO THE
RAIN

SPEAK TO THE RAIN

by Helen K. Passey

ATHENEUM   1989   NEW   YORK

Atheneum
Macmillan Publishing Company
866 Third Avenue, New York, NY 10022
Collier Macmillan Canada, Inc.
First Edition
Designed by Barbara A. Fitzsimmons
Printed in the United States of America
10 9 8 7 6 5 4 3 2 1

Library of Congress Cataloging-in-Publication Data
Passey, Helen K.
Speak to the rain/by Helen K. Passey.
—1st ed. p. cm.
Summary: In the wake of her mother's recent death, Janna's senior
year in high school becomes a time of horror, as her father starts
to drink heavily and her nine-year-old sister is possessed by the
restless spirits of an entire tribe of drowned Indians, crying out
sorrowfully to be led into the next world.
ISBN 0-689-31489-2
[1. Supernatural—Fiction. 2. Alcoholism—Fiction. 3. Death—
Fiction. 4. Single-parent family—Fiction. 5. Indians of North
America—Fiction.] I. Title.
PZ7.P2694Sp 1989 [Fic]—dc19
89-6632 CIP AC

FOR ALL MY STORYTELLER MIDWIVES—THANKS

SPEAK TO THE RAIN

PROLOGUE

Night folded quietly down, layer upon layer obscuring the isolated village. Smoke from the cooking fires drifted close above the river, barely visible in the failing twilight. Mingling with the sharp resinous smell of the great fir trees, it eddied through the air, carrying the presence of the village far down the wind.

Close to the old waterline, a single figure stood quietly in the dusk, looking down at the water. Bulky robes swathed the form, and with every movement deer hoof rattles clattered quietly. Even the night wind seemed to know the power of the shaman, and parted without touching him.

The river twisted in a narrow channel between wide tumbled banks, a living thing wasting away in sickness. It pushed weakly toward the sea and freedom, slipping listlessly past the huddled buildings. When the earth had grumbled and the water fell, the men had laughed. Raven had shaken the earth, and now he sought to hold back the rivers as well. It was a good joke, a trick worthy of the great Trickster, and the men laughed their

1

appreciation. But the water did not rise. Did Raven think to hold the river forever?

In time the laughter turned grim, and by now had long since ceased. Three summers had passed, and with each the salmon had been fewer. Starvation walked among them in the winter months, unhindered, an unfamiliar specter in a land of plenty. Singling out a child here, a grandmother there, even a warrior or hunter when it chose, it took its toll. Now there were only fifty-seven left of their clan.

Tomorrow, they would leave this place to Raven and his bitter joke. It was a long journey back to the coast, and those others awaited them there, the men with skins like unbaked dough and iron sticks that coughed out death. It was a dangerous course, but perhaps it would not be too late to fill the food boxes. They had been careful, returning every scrap and every bone to the water from whence it came, that the salmon might be reborn to come again the following season. When the child had drowned, they had sung the songs and danced the dances to show him the way, that he might go to the village of the salmon people to tell of their hunger. They had cleansed themselves to restore the balance of the world and make things right again. And now they waited.

The sounds of activity from the cedar longhouse gradually died, and quiet settled like a blanket over the narrow valley. A child cried briefly, and was silenced, and at last only the voices of the men who gambled by the fire could be heard murmuring through the night. When they crept to their beds the longhouse grew dark. Still the shaman stood, waiting for a sign in the darkness. A white owl drifted on the currents of the night hunt, and at last the sign was given. A cry, a name in the voice of the owl. His own name. Only that one sound, then the silence of the night. So be it. The Guardian always knew who next would be touched by death, and from his calling there was no turning back. Tomorrow there would be a funeral, dancing and deer hoof rattles, and he would be led to the world beyond by a new shaman. It was well. The courtesy had been given, that he might not meet death unaware and without courage. Satisfied, he sought his sleeping place.

The river, winding down from the mountain far away, spoke to the stars, and branches sighed in a slight breeze. A shower of sparks scattered upward through the smokehole as the fire was stirred and tended by its lone guard. The feeble light washed down the backs of the crest poles standing before the village and across the great near-completed totem that lay by the side of the longhouse. It grinned briefly in the flare of light, unfinished, waiting.

The guard nodded, his head sinking toward his chest. There was no one to hear as the owl cried again and again, never repeating. Fifty-seven names in all, then the telling was done, and the night drew down deeper. In the bottomless hush the dogs began to stir and whine, testing the air, uneasy. The guard dozed by the fire.

When Raven shook the earth, he did it slyly. A bare thread of sound grew on the wind, and the ground seemed to swell. Then a deep-throated roar burst out of the dark, and the earth rose and fell in waves, tossing the houses like canoes on rough seas. The dogs slunk out, and voices cried fearfully, the sound absorbed by the thrashing forest all around. Then the pitching of the earth rumbled down into a slow decrescendo, ending at last with a single shudder, and silence. Even the river had gone quiet. Within the longhouse there was confusion and the sounds of mothers comforting their children. There was no more movement of the earth. It stood still, and at last all sound from the longhouse ceased. Only the dogs stood outside, heads up and bodies tense.

As one they turned and fled up the valley side.

Far up the mountain, in the near-absolute dark of a deep canyon, the silence did not return. Shards of the canyon lip bounced dully down the slope in the wake of a larger rockfall, and the very ground moaned. What remained of the river channel after the last earthquake was now sealed, and the building pressure weakened something deep in the dam. A shattering report rang against the walls of rock, echoing to the sky, and there was a shifting in the dark. Water gleamed faintly where only shadow had lain. The river gnawed at its barriers. Freeing itself at last, the river exploded outward into a raging torrent. It funneled down the canyon, a solid grinding wall of destruction.

Raven's dam had burst.

The village met its doom in sleep. One hoarse cry of alarm speared across the swelling roar of the water and was swallowed as the longhouse disappeared. The village totems were snapped off, tossed high by the flood and carried far up on its breast. Just beyond the clearing the valley narrowed with an outthrust of rock, and the load of debris jammed against this and the water slowed. No longer held by the torrential force, the rocks and mud began to settle out rapidly. Some of the trunks and crested poles caught against the upper edge of this dam and were pushed and held upright, to stand drunkenly against the sky, while others snagged against their bases or tumbled over the top of the barrier. Water continued to pour across the wall for some time, a sleek heavy current that sifted silt into the deepest cracks as it ran down to the original riverbed. Even that slowed at last, until only a small trickle of stream pushed over the top and washed down the new slope beyond.

The night was fading when silence returned to the place where the village had been. A wide sheet of water stretched away into the dark, lapping against the trunks of the trees that climbed the steep valley sides, soothing the hidden dead. An empty carved box popped up out of the water and eddied toward the outlet. Nothing else moved.

The unfinished crest pole stood at one end of the newly formed dam, pinned precariously upright. As the stars began to disappear into the paling sky it swayed, creak-ing, and at last fell heavily across a half-buried boulder. The pole broke in two, and the lower portion rolled a single slow turn away from the water and came to rest, halted by some obstruction. Sightless wooden eyes stared away toward the sea in an eternal frozen grimace.

In the cooling darkness of the dead they waited, sep-arate and patient, for the calling that would bring them across the boundaries of the world. Then the wind bent down and touched the water, and its shiver reached deep, prying, pulling. One by one they were torn loose, naked spirits mewing under an empty sky. Who? Who will lead us there? The wind stirred almost-shadows together as they whispered again, Who?

The ghost-door stood open before them, and beyond it the fearful nothing between the worlds. Someone would come. Someone to sing the songs and call the names before the numbered moons ran out and the ghost-door closed and sucked them into unlife. Someone . . .

The white owl drifted low, to land on the broken totem and chirr softly once into the fading night. Deer hoof rattles seemed to clatter in the air before the wind died, dissolving the not-quite-shadows against the water. The stillness was absolute once more, a questioning si-lence surrounding the lake that lay gray in the beginning dawn.

SHE WASN'T GOING TO LIKE IT HERE.
Janna stood in the open doorway and looked around
the empty living room. Smudged walls, cobwebs on
the ceiling. The house breathed a heavy odor of
smoke, mildew, and emptiness.

Walking across the gritty, ugly carpet, Janna tried
to imagine their own belongings in the dingy room.
She couldn't even envision herself in this place, here
and now. Instead she saw the house Mom had kept
so nearly spotless. After all this time, her mind still
edged away from the thought. Mom.

Janna nudged one of the drapes experimentally,
then coughed in the swirl of dust. "This dump'll
take forever to clean, Karen." There was no answer.
Janna glanced at her sister, standing quietly in the
doorway. The more work, the better. Maybe it
would help pull Karen out of her hell of self-blame.
She was only nine. Janna stared out at the overcast
sky and the dark evergreens ringing the house and
drew a frowning face on the murky pane.

7

A muffled, glassy clinking reached her from out-side. Dad was unloading the car, top priority first. The bourbon. His ticket out of hell came in bottles.

She pushed away from the window and went on into the kitchen. It was even worse, big and out of date, painted a sickly off-yellow. Janna looked in disgust at the grimy countertops and the crusted sink. She hated the room on sight. The backyard wasn't much either, just a narrow mossy strip be-yond the rickety porch, dim through the dirty window. A few ragged blades of grass struggled through the choking moss and seemed to cringe away from the dense evergreens that rose behind the house.

The trees dominated everything, a stiff wave threatening to overwhelm the meager clearing. The hills swelled and buckled under their weight, mile on mile, ever higher. It was supposed to be one of the last major tracts of virgin timber in Washington State, and only the highest peaks shook free at last of the deep green tide. Janna felt suffocated. Back home in Montana the wind had silvered the sage-brush and rolled across the wide spaces. Here the dark trees loomed across the sky and raked the wind to nothing. Deep shadow moved stealthily at the edge of sight, motion that stopped when she turned toward it. Swaying beyond her vision, the shadows drew her to look even deeper into the unfamiliar woods. Janna shivered and tore herself away, turning her back on that vast living stillness. Like the afterimage of a bright light, she could still see the trees, feel them crowding the window behind her.

Karen hadn't moved from the living room, her eyes, too, following the creeping shadows. Janna put a hand on her shoulder.

"Let's go upstairs and look at our room, Kare."

Her sister turned around with a dull expression. She looked pinched and old. "All right." Karen walked away toward the stairs.

Janna stood a minute longer, gazing blankly after her. It wasn't like her sister to be so automatically obedient, and she was thinner. Her lively spirits had dissolved into dark-circled eyes and long silences. Karen was gradually drifting away, and one thought went with Janna up the stairs. She didn't know how to bring her back.

The bedroom was big, but that was the only good thing about it. Stained paper peeled away from the walls, too faded to be any certain color. The house had been a family joke, once. Dad had inherited it years ago when a great-uncle died and, unable to rent or sell, had kept it. Now they had to live here, and it wasn't funny anymore. Janna pulled on a long strip of wallpaper and let it flutter to the floor.

"I bet Dad will let us paint the room after we get this off," she said, trying to draw her sister out. "What color do you want, Karen?"

Her sister didn't answer, and Janna tried again. "Where do you think you'd like your bed? I'll give you first pick."

9

Karen shrugged, poking with her foot at a pile of shredded paper on the floor. Probably a mouse's nest. "In the corner, I guess. Maybe."

Janna gave up and wandered to the window again. Their room overlooked the lane and the sloping front yard, and beyond them the mountains stood solid and silent. The wall of evergreens was farther away here, but somehow even more compelling. Pushing and pulling, they buffeted her inner senses, waiting even as they repelled her as a stranger. Her eyes strayed again and again toward a single point, where two knifeback ridges pinched a narrow valley between them. There seemed nothing remarkable about the spot, but an unaccountable tingle scurried down her back. "There's not another house in sight. Nothing but the woods."

Karen pressed up close to her side. She looked out the window briefly, then up at Janna. "What's out there, Janna?"

"Just trees, I guess, and wildlife." Janna's eyes were pulled toward that valley again.

Karen turned and surveyed the dirty ceiling and the faded walls. "Why would Daddy make us live in a house like this, Janna? I liked the old one."

"It was Mom's house," Janna said, and felt Karen pull away, collapsing back into herself. She took her sister's face in her hands and tried to look her in the eyes, but Karen kept her gaze riveted on Janna's left ear. "It's not your fault, Kare."

The silence was leaden. Not a muscle moved in Karen's face. At first she had tried to talk about it, aching for reassurance that Dad didn't blame her. It never came. Deep in his own grief, he had sidled away from any mention of Mom. Now Karen always did too, giving her own interpretation to his silence. Janna sighed, and let her go. Karen thumped along behind her down the stairs, and ran outside.

Dad was in the kitchen, lounging against the counter and jingling the car keys in his pocket. "I got the worst of the stuff out of the garage, but we won't be able to put the car away until I fix the door. Thought I'd go back into town and pick up some lumber and nails and see what I can do with it."

Janna nodded. "Sure. There are some things I could get at the market."

He shifted uneasily. "I thought maybe you girls would be all right here at the house. . . . " His intention dangled between them. After the long, dry drive, he wanted a few drinks in town with company. It was a familiar pattern.

"But what about dinner?" she protested.

He smiled crookedly, and the gray fatigue fell away from his face. Dark hair, startling green eyes, olive complexion—he had stamped both girls with his image. "I'll check out the local hamburger joint on the way home."

It would be useless to argue. He'd just shrug and say sorry, as though that ended it.

"We'll be all right, I guess," Janna said resentfully. She didn't want to stay alone with Karen in this trash pile, much less clean it. A little arson seemed like a better idea.

"I'd better get going, then. I'll be back in an hour or two." Fat chance, she thought. She never let herself depend on his promises anymore. He started toward the door, then turned back, frowning. "And you leave that sack alone. I'll take care of it when I get back."

Janna threw a quick guilty glance at the bag of liquor. He knew. She must have dumped a few too many back home.

"It'll keep disappearing if you keep buying." The words were out before she could stop herself. An angry silence thunderclapped between them and shattered under her father's explosion.

"Damn it, Janna, back off! I can handle my own life." Sudden anger darkened his face, twisted his mouth into a bitter line. She felt she barely knew her father now. "Quit poking into things that don't concern you."

"But it's our life, too, Dad," she reminded him, repressing the shake that tried to creep into her voice. For a moment Janna wished she could take it back, but she stood her ground. She was tired of skirting things, of pretending everything was fine. Nothing was fine. Time stretched thin as they stood facing each other, until her father's features began to relax.

"Yeah. It's your life too. And the three of us, we're all we've got, right?" A wry, self-mocking smile crossed his face. "Everything's okay."

He reached out in a sudden, brief gesture and touched her hair gently. "You worry too much, JJ. I'm taking care of you." Then as though his words had scraped a nerve, he jerked away. When he spoke again, over his shoulder, his voice had roughened. "I'll bring you those hamburgers."

Janna stood in the kitchen long after the trees had swallowed the sound of his car.

2

BY THE FIRST DAY OF SCHOOL, THEY were finally moved in. Janna kicked at the last of the empty moving boxes piled on the porch and closed the door behind her, sighing. It was no good wishing they didn't have to go.

The sun was just topping the towering evergreens, barely reaching into their clearing and beginning to warm the air. "Come on, Karen, it's time to go."

Karen stood at the edge of the porch, struggling with the buttons on her sweater. "Okay." She looked even paler this morning, as she obediently moved after Janna and abandoned her buttoning efforts.

Together they walked across the lawn and entered the shade beneath the trees where the lane cut through. The underlying chill of the morning dropped around them, seeping under Janna's collar and up her sleeves. The potholed drive curved off through the woods, the surging undergrowth on either side forcing them to walk single file down the hummocky center strip. It would be a long half mile to the road.

At the bottom of the deep slash through the trees, they passed in and out of thin dribbles of light that pierced the pressing evergreens. It was almost perfectly still, hardly a breath of air finding its way so far down. The woods seemed impenetrable, a solid wall of limbs and trunks and undergrowth.

High above, the branches dipped and bobbed gently, but not here. Only once did a skein of breeze loop around them, pulling at the branches, and on it came a vague feeling, like a far-off cry. Janna heard nothing but the sudden rushing of the wind, but Karen spun slowly on her heel, looking searchingly at the wall of tangled growth. As Janna watched, Karen stopped, and walked forward until she stood at the very edge of the trees, reaching out to touch a low branch. A single maple leaf, edged with early red, shook loose and fell to the ground as the wind died. Still Karen listened into the quiet, her face closed.

In sudden, unexplained apprehension Janna laid an arm across Karen's shoulders. "Come on, let's go."

"It's almost like I can hear something. Out there." Karen looked up and smiled, an uncertain expression on her face. She hadn't smiled much lately. "Someone. Someone lonely, like me."

A tendril of fear lay curled in her stomach long after that strange breeze died, and wound itself through her day. Janna tried to shove the memory

15

away. Imagination, she told herself, and kept repeating it like some catechism of common sense. Eventually, the feeling faded under the pressures of the first day in a new school.

Karen was too nervous to go alone, so Janna had to get off at the elementary and take her in. Between getting Karen settled and walking across town to the high school, Janna missed her first class and part of her second. She felt a wash of bitterness against her father as she collected her late slip. He should have been taking care of Karen instead of sleeping off half a bottle of bourbon.

As the day ground on, Janna wished she were still in Montana. The pretest her music teacher had given had shown her to be far ahead of the rest of the kids. And when Janna went up to ask him after class, he'd said there wasn't a private flute teacher within thirty miles. The science room was primitive, her chemistry teacher sounded bored. And as a stranger in a small town, she felt shut out, excluded. Except for Kyle, a few curious glances were all she got.

Kyle was different. He'd climbed onto the bus at the next stop after theirs that morning and dropped into the empty seat in front of them as though he owned it.

"Hi," he said, slewing around to face them. "You must be the ones living up at the old Kelvin place. Your name's Miles, right? I'm Kyle Heston."

For a long moment Janna just stared at him. "How did you know?" she managed at last.

16

He grinned, "Nothing to it, just the small-town grapevine. You're a senior, aren't you?"

His friendliness had seemed astonishing then, but during the day Janna had learned that there wasn't anyone in the school that Kyle didn't appear to be good friends with. He was greeted with genuine liking everywhere.

By the end of the second week, she felt as though she had known him forever. And nothing else had really changed.

Janna dropped into a hard vinyl seat on the bus and leaned her head against the window, glad to be on her way home. Kyle's tall figure came down the aisle and flopped into the seat in front of her. He arranged himself across it with a familiar grin.

"I see you survived the surprise quiz."

"Barely," Janna said. Responding to the open, friendly blue eyes, she smiled. "I thought I might dry up and blow away during English lit, though."

"In the blast of hot air from old lady Burke, that sounds natural. Only thing that kept me awake was Ronnie's snoring." He swept the straight, brown hair away from his forehead. "You seem to be starting out pretty well in Mark's class, though."

"I'd have to work at it not to, with him teaching," Janna replied with warmth. Mark Nestor was young, medium height with a homely, open face, and good-humored eyes. He taught the advanced math classes with a lively enthusiasm that stood out among the overworked small-town teachers, and most of his

17

students just called him Mark. "A little place like this is lucky to have him. He could be teaching anywhere."

"I know. I asked him once why he stayed, when he could get better pay somewhere else. Mark said he wasn't needed just anywhere, but here." There was respect in Kyle's voice, and admiration. "He can spend a lot of time on the reservation, too, working with the Indian activists, tutoring the kids, and collecting legends."

"Legends? Why?"

"Mark's writing a paper, something about the relationship between Indian beliefs and psychic research. And you should see his collection of Northwest Indian art. It's fantastic."

Janna looked at him questioningly. "You know him pretty well, don't you?"

"Yeah. We've worked together on a lot of extra credit math, and I went with him to a couple of native religion seminars in Seattle." Kyle shot her an unreadable gaze, then shrugged. "I've stayed there a few nights when things got rough at home, too, when my dad was out of work. Mark does that kind of thing for people." Abruptly, he shifted the subject, as though unwilling to go any further in that direction. "Think you'll make it through the old fire-breather's assignment this week?"

"You mean lit? Only if I'm lucky." Janna relaxed into the seat as they talked.

18

When the bus sighed to a halt at the elementary school, Janna tensed. She couldn't see Karen at first. The children waited in chattering, shifting groups, but her sister wasn't in any of them. Janna spotted her at last and sank back against the seat. Karen was a single island of stillness, alone and aloof. She looked pale and unhappy as she walked back and climbed across Janna's knees to the window.

"How'd your day go, Kare?"

Kyle tweaked a strand of hair. "Hi, Karen."

"Hi. It was all right, I guess. For a dumb school."

"Maybe you'll like it better after a while." Karen said nothing. After a moment she pulled a book from her bag and laid it in her lap. She held it open, but stared out the window, eyes turned to the sky.

Janna glanced helplessly at Kyle, who shrugged.

The bus made its halting way along the highway, grinding out the miles from town. With every stop it became emptier and quieter. Janna was barely paying attention to the passing scene, until something familiar caught her eye.

"We passed your stop," she said.

Kyle nodded. "Yeah. I asked Tom to let me off at yours. I wanted to show you something."

"What?"

"You'll see," he answered with a grin. The bus lurched to a halt, and Kyle jumped up. He waited and followed them down the steps, then started away from the lane along the road's edge as the bus

19

coughed off in a cloud of diesel fumes. Turning on his heel and walking backward, he called out, "Come on."

Karen looked up at Janna uncertainly, then ran to follow him, dark hair flying. For the moment the deepening apathy seemed to have dropped from her. Janna closed her eyes briefly and willed it to last.

Kyle stopped a short distance down the road, and Janna caught up with them there. On the other side of the drainage ditch lay a narrow gap in the heavy undergrowth, a faint trail of packed earth threading through it.

"I got to thinking maybe you don't know yet about the trail," he said as Janna came up to them. "I used to come this way a lot when old man Kelvin was alive. It's a lot shorter, since the lane curves out around a gully and this goes straight across above it."

"Where does it go?" Karen asked, eyes sparkling with interest.

"To your house, short stuff. It's the scenic route." He grinned over her head at Janna. "I'll walk you."

Janna hesitated. The woods seemed so dark and dense, so alive. And as much as she had tried to bury it, she remembered Karen's odd feeling that something—someone—was out there. Someone lonely. Janna shook off a shiver, intending to refuse the shortcut, and then she looked at her sister. Karen was bright and eager, the life in her eyes softening the pinched shadows of her face. Janna swallowed her objections.

"I'd like that," she said instead.

"All right!" Kyle pushed in first, holding back the heavy elderberry branches and letting them whip into place once they were through. For the first time, Janna was really inside the woods.

Her first sensation was of time dripping from the limbs, oozing from the ground. Age hung heavy around them. There were giants here that had never felt the ax. Along the slash of the road the undergrowth was thick, but it quickly trickled to occasional sun-starved patches of spindly green. Trunks and limbs—dead, dying, and living—crowded around them. Off the trail the ground was a confused tangle of broken branches and half-buried logs, the undisturbed detritus of years.

Janna craned her neck to look up, but only the tiniest splinters of sky rewarded her effort. The stillness of the air around them was almost absolute, in contrast to the endless shifting of the highest branches. They made a dry, secret sound, thousands of witnesses whispering together.

Karen ran ahead as though she knew where she was going, and Janna started to call her sister back. Kyle's touch stopped her.

"She'll be all right." His hand dropped from her arm again, and he smiled apologetically. "I don't mean to tell you how to handle your sister, but she seems to have come out of her shell now. I think you should encourage it."

It was a temptation to resent his suggestion; she'd

been more or less raising Karen for the better part of a year. Janna gave him a long look, then shrugged. He was right. "I guess she's safe enough. She'll probably just crawl back into herself later. She always does." Janna kicked at an inoffensive clump of earth. He was a friend, or at least she hoped so, but she was still alone. In the last two weeks Janna had avoided the subject of her family. Kyle knew nothing of their situation. She didn't think he'd turn away, but you never knew. Janna had had a bitter lesson in that already. One of her best friends had dropped her after the accident, suddenly uncomfortable in her company. And many of the others had been alienated by Janna's own depression after her mother's death. She was determined not to let that happen here.

Not yet, she thought; she wouldn't tell him yet.

They walked along silently for a time, single file. The trail was a narrow thread of hard earth beneath their feet. It was Kyle who spoke first.

"I thought your dad must be a logger or something, since that's what everybody else does around here, but now I'm not so sure. For one thing, you don't talk like a logger's kid." Kyle grinned. "You should have seen your face when Leanne said her father was a choker setter. So, what's your dad do?"

"What is a choker setter, then?" Janna countered, hoping to fend off the question. Not yet. She didn't want to go into any of that yet. She wanted to hold

22

on to this time, and Kyle's friendship, apart from reality.

"I thought so. A choker's the chain that goes around a log so it can be dragged up to the truck, and a setter puts it there. It's dangerous work." He prodded her shoulder from behind with one finger. "You're evading me, Janna. What is he, a hit man or something?"

"Hardly. He's just not working, okay? Not until he drinks up the money from the house, anyway." Bitterness had crept into her voice before she could stop herself from saying too much. Kyle, behind her, didn't answer, and Janna felt compelled to go on. "He sold insurance until Mom was killed, then he quit. All that stuff about security is just lies. The money doesn't change anything."

This time his hand on her arm pulled her to a halt, gently.

"Hey, I'm really sorry about your mother. I didn't mean to pry." Janna couldn't meet his eyes. Afraid to see pity, the rejection she might find, she looked past him. "Karen's still getting over it?" he asked.

She bit her lip, and nodded slowly, keeping her eyes fixed on a branch beyond Kyle's shoulder. "Karen was there, in the car. She thinks she caused the accident."

He exhaled heavily, whistling through his teeth. "And did she?"

Janna felt the trembling start in her knees and

gulped down a deep breath. Her stomach was a tight knot. "I don't know. Nobody knows. . . . " She wouldn't cry. Not here, not now. "Karen didn't kill her! They were just in the wrong place at the wrong time."

Kyle's hands gripped her shoulders, and Janna dared to meet his eyes. She saw only concern. No pity. No anger. "I'm sorry. That's a hard way to lose someone."

"I was supposed to be driving."

"That doesn't make it your fault either." He looked thoughtfully down the trail to where Karen's red windbreaker was just visible through the trees. "I bet it all falls to you, too."

"Sometimes," she admitted. He hadn't left her, then, hadn't suddenly remembered he had to be home. No heavy-handed awkward apologies, and for that Janna was grateful. The tension left her body, and the grief subsided again below the surface of her mind. Janna stepped away from him. They walked on, following the bright splash of Karen's jacket.

Ahead of them the sunlight grew stronger, pouring down into a break in the woods. As Janna passed through the fringe of undergrowth, she could see Karen standing on a massive fallen log, and beyond her the gleam of water.

As soon she spied them, Karen waved and called, "Janna, look, it's a lake! Come on!"

24

3

THE LAKE WAS A PLACE OF HAUNTING beauty. Golden shallows shaded quickly to a deep blue-green where the bottom dropped away, clear as a sheet of colored crystal. Drowned timber fringed the shallows, silver-gray wood and pale moss etched bright against the dark backdrop of the evergreens.

The water reflected a blaze of sunlit sky, but somehow Janna sensed behind the brightness an elemental dark. There was something different here. She felt conflicting emotions stir, fear and dislike and an uneasy fascination.

Kyle stood close to the huge dead log where Karen was standing above the water, teasing her about falling in. He seemed ready, though, to grab her if she should slip. Sure her sister was safe enough, Janna wandered toward the water.

This entire end of the lake was choked with dead trees, standing, leaning, lying in a crisscrossed maze under the water. As the sunlight flickered down through the water, Janna seemed to see cruel parodies of faces, melting and shifting with the shadows below.

"Hey, Janna, watch this!" Kyle's voice made her look around. "I taught Karen this throw. She does it pretty good."

Janna forced herself to watch and laugh and comment on Karen's skill, but something else had caught her attention. When she had turned, her eyes swept naturally up the vertical wall of the trees, to the twin ridges shouldering against the sky. This was that narrow fold in the hills they could see from their window, which pulled and repelled her.

Karen dropped a stick into the tangled depths at her feet, where the bottom fell away in an almost vertical line. A ripple wrinkled its way across the surface, lapping gently at the standing wooden corpses, throwing off pale splinters of light to fracture the familiar shading of her face. Janna watched in sudden uneasiness, seeing a change in Karen's eyes, feeling a stir in the air. It glided from the lake, touched her, and passed on, gone as the ripples subsided.

Janna turned away abruptly. "Let's go, Kyle. I don't like this place."

He swung Karen down and guided her toward a trail on the far end of the tiny beach. "What's wrong?"

She looked over her shoulder, out across the water. It was still as glass, and that odd, vague impression was gone. Something white fluttered between the branches and vanished. "You don't feel anything?"

"Nothing," he said. Janna couldn't decide whether to be relieved or not.

Long after they had gotten home, the vision of the lake continued to lie in Janna's mind. Like a curtain of static it interfered with everything she tried to do. With a sigh, she finally dropped her lit book beside her on the bed. She still couldn't say why it had affected her. She didn't want to think about the lake, to keep seeing the strange patterned shadows on the old fallen trees and the water lights playing on the standing snags, or the look in Karen's eyes, a recognition and a sort of knowing sadness, as that stir in the air wrapped around them. With a sudden impatient movement, Janna went downstairs to start dinner.

Brett Miller was leaning against Janna's locker when she arrived at school the next morning. Janna had seen him often enough in her English class and had spoken to him a few times. Handsome, blond, and rugged, he was considered a talented football player—and the date of choice by half the girls in school. It only took her a couple of days to pick up on that. All the girls were talking about Brett.

He smiled confidently and slid his shoulder to the next locker so she could open her own and hang up her sweater.

"Hi, Janna. Hey, what are you doing Friday

night?" Evidently, he didn't believe in preamble.

"Not a thing." Janna looked up at him, almost afraid to hope. Was he asking her out?

"Great." He grinned and reached into her locker to steady her flute as it started to slide out of control. "They finally managed to hijack a decent movie to this town, and I wanted you to come with me. How about it?"

"Brett, that sounds great. I'd love—" The words were suddenly a choking lump in her throat. Karen. She'd forgotten, in her own sudden taste of freedom, that she couldn't go out and leave Karen home alone. Janna knew she was hesitating too long, and the decision was made almost before she realized it. "I'd love to. What time?" she heard herself saying.

She was halfway to her history class before she was jarred back to reality. A tight knot formed in her stomach as Janna realized she'd made a date she couldn't possibly keep.

For most of that afternoon she tried to convince herself that it would work. Karen should be old enough to stay by herself for one evening—and Dad might even stay home. Janna moved in a state of nervous, almost defiant excitement, but she knew it wouldn't work. Not after she came home and found Dad unshaven and sleeping in his chair, with a half-empty glass still in his hand. He wouldn't stay home, not on a Friday night. Janna couldn't leave Karen alone.

Twice she started to call Brett, and twice she put

the phone down with the number only half-dialed. What could she say that would sound halfway convincing? Nothing. Janna replaced the receiver.

She still didn't know what to say Friday afternoon, when she was finally able to get a few minutes with him. He'd stopped by her locker again after the last bell.

"Ready for tonight?" he drawled, leaning against the locker next to hers.

"Brett, I—" Even for a few hours, there was no escape from the distorted patterns of her life. Janna took a deep breath and tried once more. "I can't go."

Brett straightened up, standing away from the locker. His eyes narrowed, and she thought he suspected she was playing with him. "I thought you said you were free?"

Gripping the locker door, the cold metal gnawing at her fingers and palm, Janna tried to explain. "I have to stay home."

"This is a great time to tell me! What's the matter, won't your parents let you come?" There was sarcasm in his voice, and Janna flinched. She knew she deserved some of his anger, for not telling him sooner.

"It isn't that." It was useless to try to explain. She'd made a total mess out of it. Staring intently at nothing in particular inside her locker, Janna said miserably, "I'm sorry, Brett. I really wish I could have gone."

"Yeah, I bet." He shifted his books from one hand

29

to the other, and his eye seemed to catch on some passing face. His anger was replaced with a sudden impatience. "Hey, look, I gotta go. See ya around."

"Sure," she answered, though she knew he couldn't hear her through the crowd. Janna watched him dart between several other students and catch up with Candi Gannet. Giving the door a resounding slam, she spun the lock and raced for her bus. The cold of the locker door lingered in her palm.

Fall was making itself felt that week for the first time. A finger of storm had reached out from the north Pacific and brushed the coast, and almost overnight the vine maples flamed into scarlet highlights on the hillsides. Clouds layered over the clear sky, dimming the light, piling against the mountains. The gray light matched Janna's mood that afternoon. The first cold drops of rain fell before she and Karen reached the house, bringing a strange quiver to the air.

Janna went straight up to her room, not wanting to talk to anyone, and slammed the door. Pulling off her wet shoes, she threw them hard at the wall. The double thump wasn't loud enough to be satisfying, and she flopped down on her bed.

Why had she ever said yes to Brett? It had been a dumb move, but she had wanted to get away so badly. Janna punched her pillow and sat up. Brett would never ask her again, and there was nothing she could do about it now. She reached for her homework.

Outside the rain went on and on, calling Janna. It pulled her restlessly to the window, willed her to gaze toward the ridges and feel a lost aching. It leached the color from the trees and the grass, pulled the sky down low to brush the ridges, and beat a lilting staccato rhythm against the house. Somehow it made her think of the lake, and Janna took up her flute to bury the sound.

Lisping the day and the night together into a single long, toneless sentence, the rain began to feel like a presence, a vast personality brooding in the gathering dark. It waited and it muttered to itself, and the feeling it carried to Janna was the same as she had felt at the lake. By the time dinner was over and she could finish her homework, Janna wished it would stop, take its sly whispering away over the mountains and leave her alone.

"Karen, quit!" Janna snapped and pushed irritably at the grubby sheet of paper that was sliding across her own. She'd been trying for over an hour to get this one problem right. The paper was withdrawn, but Karen didn't move. She stood by her shoulder, eyes downcast. Janna sighed. It wasn't Karen's fault, any of it. "What now?"

"I forgot how you showed me." Karen's voice was listless, tired. "I tried and tried, honest."

"I'm sorry, Kare. I know you did. Here, it's like this." Janna scribbled a set of numbers on another piece of paper. "I thought Dad was going to help you with your homework."

31

"He said he would."

"Well, I can't do yours and mine, too, Karen. Go find Dad, have him help you." The resentment was back, a slow burning in her mind, and she shoved the paper roughly back at her sister. How could he do this to them? He knew good old Janna would take up the slack, that's how. Well, not this time.

"I think he found that bottle." Karen lifted her eyes to meet Janna's blank stare and added helpfully, "You know, the one in the storeroom, under the old papers. He's in sleeping by the fireplace."

She should be used to it by now, but still it filled her with bitter disappointment. Each day Janna hoped for a change, almost willing things to get better—and each day crumbled her hopes. Even with her father at home, Karen would have been on her own tonight if Janna had gone out with Brett.

"Never mind. Try the next one, okay?" She kept her voice as even as possible for Karen. Everything for Karen.

Her homework seemed remote, meaningless, and she put it away. She could never keep up anyway.

Dropping her chin into her hand, Janna stared unhappily at the window. It was a solid, reflective square, shutting out the enveloping trees and the night that was closing down on them.

The sound of the front door closing and her dad's voice reached her from the living room. Who could

32

be coming here? Janna turned just as Kyle came into the kitchen, followed by her father.

"Hi." Pushing his dripping hood back, Kyle grinned at her. "I got stuck with my homework. Want to give me a push?"

Janna watched in an agony of embarrassment as her dad slapped Kyle unsteadily on the shoulder, sending water splattering through the air, and leaned close. "Friend from school, eh? Didn't hear you drive up." The words slurred together.

Janna moistened suddenly dry lips. "This is Kyle, Dad. He lives down the road." She wanted to drop through the floor.

"Hello, Mr. Miles." Kyle put out his hand, and Janna's father looked from it to his own in apparent confusion. His palm was still wet from that hearty clap on Kyle's shoulder. Finally he wiped it dry on his pants and shook Kyle's hand, looking mildly pleased with himself.

"Glad'a meet you. Live aroun' here, huh?"

Janna interrupted before Kyle could reply. "We have a really tough assignment to work on, Dad."

"Hey, don' mind me." Her dad nodded, and settled against the door frame, running his hand through his hair until it stood up in sloppy spikes. He yawned, then raised his wrist and focused blearily on his watch. "Karen's bedtime a'ready. G'on now, baby."

Karen looked questioningly at Janna, chewing on

her eraser. It was early yet, but Janna nodded, and Karen gathered up her books and papers and scooted toward the stairs. In the other room the TV chattered inanely to itself.

Her father's slur had already become more pronounced, the alcohol seeping deeper into his brain. Embarrassed, desperate, Janna drew Kyle's attention to herself, hoping he wouldn't notice the red she could feel washing her cheeks.

"I was really having trouble with that assignment Mark gave us. Maybe we should start with that," Janna babbled, already opening her math book.

Dropping his wet backpack onto the table and moving to a chair, Kyle nodded and picked up Janna's cue. "That's what I was hoping we could work on."

Staring vaguely at some point beyond Janna, her father interrupted them, rambling, half-coherent. He didn't seem to be talking to anyone in particular. "Can't figure it out," he muttered, shaking his head. "Can't figure it out. Ever'thing's diff'rent."

"Dad." Janna kept her voice level with an effort. She was all too aware of Kyle sitting next to her, witness to the whole pitiful scene. "Dad, don't you think you'd better go back and sit down?"

Partially recalled to his surroundings, he shifted his gaze to Janna's face and shook his head. "Nothing in there. Even th' bottle's empty."

Throat tight, her cheeks burning with mortification, Janna stared down at her book. Seeing that she

34

still held it half-open, she let the cover fall closed. It whuffed softly. Not daring to meet Kyle's eyes, she murmured, "I'll be right back."

Moving around the table, she slipped a hand into her father's arm and turned him, unresisting, back toward the other room. Once started, he went readily enough to the chair in front of the fireplace and sank down into it. Wordlessly, Janna placed a pillow behind his head, and he leaned back against it. He caught her hand as she turned to go.

"You're a lot like your mother, JJ. Not looks, 'course. Couldn't stan' that, not now." The words were barely distinguishable, his eyes already half-closed.

"Go to sleep, Dad," Janna said. A quick glance located the bottle on the floor beside the chair. As she had suspected, it was only half empty, and she picked it up cautiously, watching her father. He was asleep already.

Still not able to meet Kyle's eyes, she went to the sink and stood with her back to him. Fumbling with the cap, Janna opened the bottle and upended it over the drain. The liquor gurgled and choked as it flowed out. Confused emotions swamped her—embarrassment, pain, and a smoldering, formless anger. She wanted to curse fate, curse her mother for dying, her dad for drinking. Curse herself for living.

Kyle's chair scraped across the floor, and she turned at last. "I'm sorry, Kyle," she said helplessly.

He gestured at the bottle she still held in her hand.

35

"Are you going to catch it for dumping the rest of that?"

"No. He won't remember." Bitterness tinged her voice, tasted raw in her mouth. The smell of cheap liquor hung in the air.

"Yeah, well, don't make a big deal about it, Janna." He smiled slightly, a tight, lopsided smile. "It's nothing new to me, you know. My dad's generally crocked all weekend. His only excuse is being a logger."

"Is it bad? I mean—you know," she floundered. Kyle would understand, she thought with relief. It was something she hadn't suspected, that they shared this of all things.

Kyle shrugged. "When he's out of work things get pretty rough, with him plastered all the time. He's a mean drunk, not like yours."

Janna threw the bottle into the trash, so hard it broke. "I hate this stuff! Mom was worried about him before. He drank, but nothing like this," she said in a low voice, sitting down once more. "Not all the time."

Kyle pulled the backpack across the table toward himself, fidgeted with the damp strings. "Still feel like doing homework?"

She shook her head apologetically. "No. I'm sorry, Kyle," she said again.

"Hey, no big deal. I just hope you don't mind my barging in like this." His hands still worked the strings, tying knot upon knot. "I guess I put you in a tough spot."

"I'm glad you came." Janna's voice was beginning to come more freely, and she attempted a smile. "I was starting to feel sorry for myself."

"Because of him?" Kyle moved his head toward the living room. His eyes met hers at last, deep and unreadable. "Or for striking out with Brett?"

It had gotten around, then. Already. Janna was forced to think about it, caught by that dark gaze. "Not really Brett, I guess. I just wanted so much to get away from here for even one night. Sometimes I feel so trapped."

His eyes were suddenly shuttered. "Me too. Don't lose any sleep over Brett, okay? He's a jerk."

Janna didn't know how to reply to that and just nodded. Brett might be a jerk, but at least he'd asked her out.

Kyle stopped playing with the strings and picked the pack up by one strap. "I guess I'd better go. Maybe we can work together some other time."

Janna let her eyes meet his once more and knew that he didn't really want to leave.

"Want to make brownies or something?" she asked finally.

His sudden grin was warming, contagious. "Sure. I can do homework anytime, but brownies are something rare."

★ ★ ★

37

The whispered voice wove itself into her dreams, disturbing her, edging her toward consciousness. "Mamma? Mamma, wake up, *please*, Mamma!" Sometimes she saw Karen, heard her voice, sometimes the dream twisted back on itself until it was her own voice repeating the words, over and over. Janna's reluctant feet dragged her toward a covered stretcher, ominously large and immaculate, and she wrenched herself out of sleep, sweating. The voice went on.

"Mamma, *please*."

Disorientation gave way gradually to reality. Water chuckled through the gutters outside their window and drummed gently overhead. It was dark; no stretcher, no fading daylight and empty streets. She sat up, forcing her eyes farther open, and stumbled across the room to her sister's bed. Janna didn't know how long Karen had been pleading into the dark. She whispered soothing words, straightening Karen's quilt. "It's okay, Kare. Open your eyes, it's okay."

Karen didn't respond. Instead, she curled into a tight ball and began to sob. "She can't wake up. I killed her."

"Karen, you didn't. Come on, open your eyes."

Smoothing the sweat-dampened hair away from her little sister's forehead, Janna continued talking, trying to ease her out of the dream. Karen was always terrified if awakened too suddenly from her nightmares. Finally she sighed, and bit by bit her body relaxed. She whispered, "Janna," and then her breathing grew deep and regular once more.

The night's blackness was diluted with the coming dawn, and still Janna sat on the edge of the bed. Something tickled at her neck, and she swiped at it. It was only when she felt the damp on her hand that she realized it was tears.

There were so many images in her mind, more solid and real than the failing darkness around her. Karen, eager to leave for her slumber party. Mom slipping on her coat and saying she'd just drop Karen off on her way to the store so Janna wouldn't have to take her after all. Karen talking and laughing, her little dog bouncing at the car windows as they drove away, soundless behind the glass like a scene from an old movie. Mom, blowing a kiss from the end of the drive. Endless hospital corridors that smelled of sickness and despair, endless organ notes in a tiny chapel. White roses falling from her hand onto Mom's pale casket. The last farewell.

The investigating officer had doubted that Mom had had time to feel fear. The man driving the other car with a blood alcohol so high he could barely have been conscious had never known what he had done. For them, for Karen's little dog, a blinding instant, and nothing. For Karen, almost unhurt in the midst of death, the moment went on and on, as though it might never end. It still went on in the quiet of the night. The moment carried her to when she was finally freed from the wreckage, and it dropped her there. She had seen then. Chalk outlines on the pavement, dark stains, unmoving forms surrounded by paramedics. The rescuers had held her back as Mom was wheeled to the ambulance. "Mamma, wake up!" she'd cried. And then, as the door was slammed shut, "I killed her."

Karen had never said why she thought that, only sobbed it into the night. Bad luck or bad timing had brought them all together on that late winter afternoon. Karen had had nothing to do with it.

Janna wiped away the tears and twitched at Karen's covers again. Feeling limp and weary, she moved back to her own bed, to try and salvage something from the night. Monday morning and school were only a couple of hours away.

4

RAIN STILL POURED OVER THE HOUSE
the next morning, sheeting from the clogged gutters
and shuffling across the roof. Janna was already sick
of the dreary days and unquiet nights, of the sky
and mountains running together in a vast gray
smudge. When she and Karen stepped outside she
saw the empty moving boxes still piled by the door,
sagging with damp. She'd have to haul them out to
the garage after school. Dad would never get around
to it.

Heads down against the rain, they walked across
the front yard. The ground squelched and sucked
at their feet.

Dismayed, Janna halted when they came to the
edge of the clearing. The lane lay drowned beneath
a long squirming line of brown puddles. There was
nowhere left to walk. Reluctantly, Janna followed
Karen into the woods.

The rain didn't fall there under the trees, just
seeped and slithered toward the ground. As Janna

41

moved carefully past rain-laden branches, her sister ran far ahead.

As she followed along the trail Kyle had shown them, a vague despair stirred the air and crawled into her mind. Faltering, her feet finally slowed of themselves, and she stopped. From close beside her, a faint almost-sound like swinging rattles skirled out of the air.

Grief welled up from within her in a sudden choking flood, and behind it, a feeling like another darkness eating through, as though someone stood beside her and whispered mourning in her ear. Her thoughts were tossed up in a crazy jumble. She saw Mom, unmoving on white satin that melted into water, cold, heavy, and suffocating. She saw Karen looking out at her with dark eyes that deepened and changed, in a face that weathered and aged. And over all, there was a feeling of being alone, alone and forgotten.

Again that faint almost-sound, moving past her. A lingering sensation of presence, of a voice whispering away. Then all she felt was an aching sadness in the air. She stood by herself in the midst of the vast living blanket of Northwest forest, confused and frightened. The rain on her face recalled a wavered image of dark water, brooding. The lake. Karen was alone there by now. Janna pushed aside her own despair, and was more than half running when she finally burst out of the woods at the edge of the lake.

The rain fell steadily onto the surface of the water,

making it quiver like a living thing. It was so still that she could hear the drops hitting the water in a murmur, and the dark grief tightened inside her skull. The lake was alive and thoroughly disturbed, and the very quiet was a mockery.

All of it Janna took in as her gaze locked onto the one thing that really mattered. Karen was balanced on the old log, close above that abrupt drop-off where she had stood that day with Kyle. It would take so little, Janna realized, to send Karen down into the tangled water. Nothing more than for her to come bursting noisily out of the woods.

Janna's stomach lurched as her sister's balance deserted her and Karen teetered.

"Karen!" The trees absorbed her scream without an echo.

The gray water lay in wait, and Janna felt a sharp stab of fear. Then Karen finally lost her footing, and sat down hard astride the log. Janna was already running forward.

"Are you all right?" Concern made her voice harsh as she steadied her sister. "What if you'd fallen in?"

Karen shrugged her off. "I didn't. Just slipped in the moss. See?" She touched the gouge her heel had made as she fell, a deep slash through the spongy growth to the bright orange wood beneath.

"Well, be more careful." Janna shifted uneasily, looking across the water and then back to her sister. She remembered that strange sensation in the woods, as though she wasn't quite alone. Karen seemed to

43

feel nothing out of the ordinary, fingers busy with the loose strip of moss like any child with a discovery.

"Karen, we've got to go."

"Not yet, Janna. You should feel this. It's all bumpy, kinda." Under the moss the log was decaying and soft, but Karen brushed away the splinters of rotting wood, fingers tracing some sort of pattern. "It's a shape, like the mouth on a jack-o'-lantern."

Janna moved closer in spite of herself, lured by the excitement in Karen's voice. Her sister peeled off a larger piece of moss and dropped it, brushed more splinters away. "It's a whole face."

An unaccountable shiver prickled over Janna's skin. It was true. Karen had already uncovered the outlines of a grotesque wooden face, blurred with time, streaked with moss like living scars. It had been carved deep, however, deep enough to withstand the leveling action of the moss. Deep enough to be still recognizable.

"It looks like an old totem pole." Janna looked across the water with new vision, at the stiff snags fingering the dull sky. "I wonder if those are totems, too. If they are, there must be dozens of them."

Scattered among the standing snags, the totems were all around, tireless and straight as sentries at a prison gate. They wore their cloaks of trailing moss with a dignity lacking in the pitiful forms of the drowned trees. They were . . . different, somehow.

44

Leaning out, Janna examined the shadows on the fallen logs under the water, remembering her first impression of shapes below. They were there, slipping in and out of sight. A paw, a face, a wing, receding into the green depths. There was no sound but the patting and slithering of the rain, but for a moment Janna thought she heard something else, a soft clicking in the empty air beside her. Janna found herself sweating in sudden fear.

"Come on, let's go." Her sister was still fingering the carving, digging at the softened wood with her nails. "Stop it, Karen. We have to get out to the bus."

The younger girl's hands dropped to her sides, but she didn't move away.

"He's ugly."

"He's supposed to be ugly. Now come on," Janna repeated. Shivering under the cold touch of the rain, she started toward the road—and stopped dead at Karen's next words, her back still to the lake.

"He likes me. He wants me to stay." Something in Karen's eyes deepened as Janna looked at her. Beyond her, wings white and soft as fog fluttered between the branches. "He said so."

"I don't hear anything." Nothing but the rain, muttering against the water and lisping in the trees. Nothing. Again the wings stroked the air, and a white owl landed on a bare limb, watching them. The cold was a part of her now, inside and out, and she no longer shivered. All she wanted was away, but she had to swallow twice before she could say, "It's just old, dead wood."

Her sister didn't move. "Maybe it isn't only him, then."

Slowly Janna turned back toward the lake, Karen's thoughtful tone catching at her. "There's nobody else here."

"They're singing." At Janna's uncomprehending stare, Karen explained patiently. "You know, the voices. In the rain."

Something inside Janna grew still, as still as the carved face leering up into the streaming sky. For a moment she almost thought she heard it too, a dreary chanting all around, voices sliding and striking together like the raindrops. Then panic hit her, and she was moving. Grabbing Karen by the shoulder, she pushed her to the trail.

"No, Janna! I want to stay." Karen struggled briefly and dug in her heels. Janna shoved her forward.

"Now, Karen!" She urged her sister down the uneven trail, none too gently. Behind them the owl began to cry in the deserted clearing.

5

IN THE MIDDLE OF THE AFTERNOON THE
sullen cover of cloud broke and drifted apart, pouring out a tentative shaft of sunshine. The breach
widened steadily, and at last the storm blew inland.
A clear, washed light laid a faint polish on the tired
streets and buildings of the town and lifted even the
gloom in Janna's heart.

Kyle was leaning against the door frame, grinning,
when Janna came out of her band class.

"Hey, you play a pretty mean solo," he said by
way of greeting.

Janna felt herself color. "It was okay, I guess.
Thanks." Her mind hadn't really been on the music.

"No, really, you're good." He matched her step
as she moved down the hall toward her locker. "Will
you have that part in the concert next month?"

"I hope so, but it isn't settled yet." She opened
her locker, holding her flute awkwardly, and rummaged for her math text. "How are you doing on
all that extra credit stuff Mark gave us?"

Kyle made a face. "I wanted to ask you, how about if we get together tonight and work on it?"

"Sure," Janna said, and felt her heart lift. Kyle's company would be a good cure for an overactive imagination—a small dose of normalcy to counteract the strange experience that morning. Besides, she liked him. She liked him a lot. So it was probably best not even to mention what Karen had said at the lake, or what Janna had felt.

"Save me some homework tonight, then. About seven-thirty, if that's okay?"

Janna nodded, and felt her untidy armload of books begin to slip as she slammed her locker door.

"I'll take it that means yes," Kyle said as Janna tucked her math book back under her arm. Together they headed for the bus.

Janna's happy mood was checked when the bus stopped at the grade school and Karen dropped into one of the front seats, huddling there alone with her books. Seeing Karen made it hard to keep the memories of the lake from creeping out of hiding, but Janna clamped down hard on them. There was nothing strange at the lake. Nothing.

And they wouldn't go by there any more.

Karen must have guessed her intention. After one quick look in Janna's direction, she scurried down the metal steps of the bus and had almost disappeared into the trees by the time Janna got off. For a long minute Janna simply stood where she was, wanting to turn the other way, pushing at a fear she wouldn't admit. In the end there was nothing to do but follow. Whatever it was that drew Karen to the lake, she was responsible for her sister.

But this afternoon was different. No odd feelings reached out for her as she approached the lake, no strange images insinuated themselves into her mind. Even the owl had gone. Her half-fears never materialized at all, and Janna breathed a deep sigh of confirmed relief.

When she reached the lake Janna found her little sister kneeling in the mud next to the totem pole. The sun was brilliant on the water, warm on Janna's skin. Her muscles, tense with a dread that the morning would be repeated, relaxed as Janna watched Karen. It was an ordinary lake, nothing more.

The deception lasted only minutes. Soon a breeze touched the water, and like an icy draft, the feeling of unease spread through her once more. Janna pulled her sister up by one arm.

"Let's head for home, Karen."

Karen protested, but obeyed. Janna scooped up her sister's forgotten book bag from the ground and went on. Though she wanted to, this time she didn't run, just let the feeling push her away. Behind her the breeze died once more, and with it went that strange, undefinable breath of misery.

As she came into the house, Janna closed the door softly and leaned back against it. Karen was perched on her dad's knee, talking excitedly. He looked tired, with the washed-out appearance of someone who'd spent the day in front of the TV, but for once he seemed sober.

"It's a real totem pole, Daddy, and Indians made it. Maybe hundreds of years ago." Karen was animated, eyes bright. Time slipped, and just for a moment everything was all right.

"Hundreds, huh? And you found it." He leaned his head back against the cushion and grinned lazily. Janna wasn't sure if he was taking her sister seriously or not.

"Karen's right, it's an old totem pole," she said suddenly, moving into the room. "She was standing on it, where it sticks out over deep water, and nearly fell in this morning."

The words came by themselves. Janna hadn't meant to say anything, not now. Later, when they were alone, she had intended to tell him everything. The chances were he'd never believe her, so she said the only thing she thought he *would* believe. The one thing she thought might prompt him to forbid their going there anymore.

"Not that deep," Karen mumbled. Some of the life had gone out of her eyes, the dullness creeping back as she looked up at her father.

"Sure, peanut." Rumpling her hair affectionately, he turned to his older daughter. He hadn't taken either of them seriously. It was a small miracle that he'd listened at all.

"How was school today? Or do I dare ask?" He flashed her the engaging grin he had worn so rarely of late.

Janna moved toward the kitchen, to put her books down and start dinner. "It was all right, I guess. How about you? The interview go okay?"

Her father shifted uncomfortably and didn't answer. Janna paused behind his easy chair, frowning. She waited.

After a long minute he tilted his head back to look at her briefly, upside down, then returned his gaze to the blank TV screen. Karen looked at her with dark eyes.

"I didn't go," he muttered when the silence finally grew too heavy.

"Didn't go!" Not again. This time, she'd thought he really would.

"I wasn't qualified, so I decided there wasn't any point in it. Something else will come up." He settled deeper in his chair, closing his eyes as though ending the discussion.

Janna couldn't let it go. The knot of tension she'd felt all day finally burst.

"What do you mean, you weren't qualified?" She snatched up the paper that lay on the floor by his chair and read the circled ad quickly. "You could have walked out of there with the job if you'd just bothered to show up. We can't keep living on the money from the house forever!"

Inside Janna was screaming to herself to stop. She wanted to, wanted to back away and let her dad take care of everything, and she couldn't. Her trust was crumbling too rapidly for that. Maybe for good.

"Knock it off, Janna." Her dad scooted Karen off his knee but still didn't turn. "I've managed to keep my family reasonably well fed for the last eighteen years without your advice, so I imagine I can do it for a while longer."

Janna flinched at the biting sarcasm in his voice but couldn't back down.

"You could at least try! You *said* you were going to get a job and use the money from the house for another one so we wouldn't have to live in this dump. Instead you're drinking it," she added brutally.

"That's enough, Janna, I mean it. Shut your mouth." There was an icy edge to his voice, a warning not to push it any further. He still stared at the dead screen, but his jaw was taut, and his forearms below rolled-up sleeves were corded. With an angry, wordless exclamation, Janna threw the paper in the direction of the lifeless television and fled the room.

Her books skidded as she threw them onto the kitchen table. Loose papers skittered away, fanning out and falling to the floor. Janna gripped the back of a chair for a minute, then went over to the sink, hardly aware of what she was doing.

Pouring soap over the dirty dishes, she turned the water on hard. She didn't even care if it was hot or cold or frozen in the pipes somewhere. Her hands were moving, that was all.

In the other room the heavy silence dragged out, until Karen began to sob softly. Springs creaked, and after a while Janna heard his low voice, soothing. She was shut out, alone with her anger.

Janna stared at the blank yellow wall above the sink. It was an ugly color to paint a room, rotten and depressing. She wasn't going to cry. Not again. There'd been enough tears last spring, and they hadn't helped a bit. Nothing helped anybody—her tears or her father's booze or Karen's withdrawal. Nothing. So she told herself the stinging in her eyes came from the ugly yellow paint and blinked back the tears.

Everywhere she turned, it seemed to be waiting for her, the silence too terrible for any of them to break. To name death was to accept it, so with their silence they tried to unmake the truth.

Her father had said it just once in a dazed, unbelieving voice. The doctor's footsteps were fading down the tiled corridor, the emergency room door beside them firmly closed. Janna could still feel the pressure of his hand on her shoulder, when he'd said, "I'm sorry." He was young and nervous, unaccustomed yet to dealing in death. That was all the doctor would say about Mom. It was enough. Most of his assurances about Karen slid through her mind without a memory. Karen was alive.

Dad had said barely two words to fill the doctor's awkward pauses, just stared down at his clasped hands hanging between his knees. When the footsteps faded away entirely and they were alone with their grief, he looked blankly at the opposite wall. "Your mother's dead, Janna. She's gone." He took a deep breath then, almost a sob, as Janna shattered quietly beside him, and the silence had begun. Sober, he had never mentioned her mother since.

Janna turned off the water. She vaguely heard her father now, suggesting that Karen go up and change her clothes, and his step as he came into the kitchen. She kept her back rigidly toward him, as though she didn't know he was there. She wouldn't look at him.

"Did you have to make a scene and upset Karen?"

Great. Now it was all her fault. "Sorry," she said shortly.

He moved farther into the room, and she had to shift to keep her back toward him. He sighed, and Janna just caught the movement as he reached up to run a hand through his hair. She suddenly realized she had washed the same bowl three times, rinsed it, and put it in the drainer. Why couldn't he just go away?

He might have read her mind. "Don't bother fixing me anything to eat, Janna. I'll be going out tonight." The edge of anger had left his voice. Now he just sounded tired.

Forgetting her resolution not to face him, Janna turned around. He leaned against the door frame, hands shoved deep into his pockets, his expression an almost impossible mixture of apology and challenge. She didn't want him to go, not really, but only the wrong words would come. "Barhopping, I suppose?"

The look of apology was gone in an instant. "You can suppose anything you want, since it's really none of your business. A few drinks never hurt anybody anyway."

"Go ahead then," she said angrily. Turning her back once more, Janna plunged her hands into the cooling water. "We do just fine on our own."

"Right. And don't wait up for me this time, okay? It's absurd." He straightened and started to turn away.

"Dad?" Janna felt him pause, and the floor creaked under his weight. He was all they had. Staring at the water, she went on in a strangled voice. "Drive carefully, okay?"

"Sure. I'll drive so slow I could probably get home faster walking." The door closed behind him, and Janna stood drawing with her finger in the dissolving bubbles.

6

THE SKY REMAINED CLEAR FOR DAYS,
sunlight pouring across the hills. Each afternoon,
Karen insisted on taking the trail past the lake, and
so long as they didn't linger too long, Janna felt it
was easier just to give in. The lake was beautiful in
the sun's brightness, but still, almost too still. It
gave back the sunshine in a grudging glitter, muted
somehow, as though the lake swallowed some of the
light. When Janna looked down from Karen's log
one afternoon, she could see the sunshine glowing
in the water, the shadows reaching for it, diluting it
until it was gone.

Janna shivered and carefully climbed down. No,
the sun could never warm her here. She wasn't even
sure why she had felt a need to stand up there and
stare down into the water. Or why she hadn't told
Kyle yet about the totem poles. She had tried to
make herself talk to him, but the memory of Karen's
voices had kept her silent. With what he knew about
her family already, what would he think?

Ravaged by time, the crest pole lay there leering

56

silently at the woods. Janna steadied herself against the log, looking down at her little sister. Karen's patient fingers had now stripped the moss from several feet of fragile carving. It was the only thing she seemed to be interested in. Gently, Janna gathered her books and coaxed her sister to head for home.

But even at home she couldn't escape that frozen face. Karen had become obsessed with it and had begun to draw its likeness, covering the walls of their room with pictures in lurid colors. Hour on hour, Karen drew, until Janna felt that the face was tattooed on her memory. She wanted to burn all the pictures. A breath of sadness clung to them, an echo of the unnatural silence of the chill breeze at the lake. There was a violence in them, too, that made her uneasy, but she couldn't destroy the only outlet for Karen's suppressed grief, or whatever it was that the totem and the lake stirred within her.

Standing in the doorway of their bedroom, she watched her little sister. Every line of Karen's body spoke of concentration.

"Cartoons are on, Karen. Why don't you come on down and watch?"

"Uh-uh." Karen reached out for another crayon, a deep and disturbing red. "I'm coloring."

"You can do that later." Her sister made no response. "How about a game, then? Cards, maybe."

Karen just shook her head, and Janna gave up. Still watching her sister, she sat down on her bed and began fitting her flute together. Dad was downstairs, drinking. Each of them might as well have been alone. Like a blank sheet, the evening stretched in front of her.

Opening her music, Janna chose one of the pieces she'd been working on before they'd moved. With the first notes of the difficult sonata, Janna let herself sink into the music. By the weight of sheer concentration she hoped to slip into the past as well.

By the time the phone rang, her lip felt stiff, her fingers hot and tired. Half regretful, half relieved, she lowered the flute when her father called to her up the stairs.

"Kyle's on the phone, JJ."

Janna felt slightly disoriented, yanked so suddenly from her absorption, and she moved toward the stairs slowly. She'd been unaware of the passage of time, of anything but the music. Her mind seemed cobwebbed, until Kyle's words scoured it out like a swift-running stream.

"I'd really like to see you tonight, Janna. Mind if I come over?"

And suddenly, she no longer wanted the past.

"Come on, Karen, quit cheating," Kyle groaned.

"I wasn't cheating." The look on Karen's face was suspiciously angelic. She met Kyle's gaze for a long moment before breaking into a grin. "Okay, I fudged a little. I still win."

"Monster!" Janna said, throwing her cards onto the table beside Kyle's. She tried to sound irritated, without much success. "You can't beat her, she just changes the rules. Anybody for popcorn instead?"

"Can we caramel it? Please, Janna?" Karen had said little during the hours before dinner, withdrawn into herself, coloring. Nothing Janna had been able to do had served to distract her, until Kyle had come. Now Karen's eyes were bright, laughing even. No trace of the earlier darkness marred her glance.

"You just want to stay up late, squirt." Kyle faked a grab at her. "I know your type."

Karen giggled and ducked under the table, scooting for the living room. She dodged another feint from Kyle, disappeared around the edge of the door frame into the other room. Poking her head back into the kitchen, she said, "Caramel!" and ran in to flop in front of the TV.

"I guess we're stuck," Kyle said, spreading his hands in defeat. "Do you mind?"

Janna shook her head, reaching for a cookbook. "Anything that can make Karen happy is okay with me."

There was a burst of incongruous canned laughter from the TV in the other room, but Kyle didn't answer, and Janna turned to look at him. He met her gaze with his own, a troubled frown in his eyes.

"I've never seen Karen like that," he said thoughtfully.

Janna sighed, the happy mood suddenly wearing thin. "She was always like that, Kyle. Mom called her her sunshine baby." There was a short silence. "At least Mom never knew her like this."

"Maybe time is all she needs," Kyle said. His eyes were uncertain, and Janna didn't think he believed that any more than she did.

Just then Karen burst into the room, full of questions about the popcorn, and Kyle scooped her up to tickle her. When she was breathless and struggling he finally put her down and they let her measure the sugar and butter. Without another word, they put the worries away into shuttered compartments of their minds. Now was all that mattered.

The wind came before the rain returned. For two days a wild gale whipped at the trees, pushing the dark piled clouds before it. At night Janna could hear it battering the house and tearing at the shingles, and it swept her mind clear of images of the lake as they streamed away on the arms of the storm. Without warning the wind would die into a breathless calm, then hit the walls once more like a solid object. Sleep came in uneasy snatches.

In the mornings the yard was littered with broken branches, the window panes plastered with bits of leaves and debris. A few scattered drops fell impatiently from the heavy sky, but for the most part the rain held off until the third day. Then the dark boiling clouds slowed and fell lower, and the wind wore itself out in one last brief spurt. And the rain closed in, deceptively gentle, falling straight down through the quiet air and slowly claiming everything.

Janna watched it from the bus shelter, watched as it drew a thin gray veiling over the trees that lined the road. She had felt it coming, and now the damp all around seemed to settle suffocatingly deep inside of her. Glancing at Karen, she saw that her sister was carefully pleating the corner of one of her drawings, ignoring the rain completely, even the single drip falling steadily on her shoulder.

During her classes she couldn't help glancing out at the rain. It fell straight down, beating the wind against the earth and pinning it there with its sheer weight. Its coldness seeped around her heart.

The day dragged on forever, but at last Janna climbed onto the bus home and chose a seat. Kyle dropped down next to her, giving her a good-natured push toward the window.

"Give me some room, okay?" He slouched way down and put his head against the back of the seat. "I'll take illiteracy over senior English any day. Burke's going off the deep end, if you ask me."

"I guess," Janna mumbled, not really paying attention. She was thinking about Karen, how the weather had changed her own feelings, wondering whether Karen would have retreated again.

Kyle straightened slowly beside her. "Hey, you in there, Janna?"

She colored. "I'm sorry, Kyle. I guess I was thinking about something else. What did you say?"

"Nothing important." He was looking at her with exasperation. "You're mother-henning over that sister of yours again."

"Does it show?"

"All over. In neon," he added, turning toward her and flicking a stray wisp of hair off her cheek. "So tell Dr. Kyle what's happened now."

Janna shook her head. "It sounds too crazy."

Kyle shrugged. His face stiffened slightly. "I wouldn't laugh, you know."

"It's not that, Kyle." Janna hoped she hadn't hurt him and tried to make her voice sound lighter. "I'm just not even sure what *is* bothering me. The rain, I guess," she added truthfully.

"It does that." He gave her another searching look. "I want to help, Janna, if you'll let me."

The blue eyes that met hers were serious with concern, and suddenly the rain didn't seem to matter anymore. "Thanks, Kyle, I will. Honest."

Janna and Kyle climbed down the muddy steps of the bus and crossed the road together. Karen, making long scuff marks in the gravel, was ahead of them, nearly at the trail.

"Wait up, Karen," Janna called. She didn't want Karen to run off alone.

Her little sister stopped reluctantly, turned and stood watching as they approached. Behind her the dark trees went up and up, and Karen's jacket was

62

a single bright fleck of life against that somber background. Her bangs were flattening on her forehead below her hood, rain streaming past her eyes. Backing another step, she looked from Janna to Kyle, turned, and ran.

"Karen!"

"Leave me alone!" The younger girl leaped the ditch and disappeared. Janna sent a small stick crashing into the brush after her.

"I just don't want her at the lake by herself."

Kyle took her hand again. "Come on, then, before she gets too much of a head start."

Janna hung back for one long moment before entering the woods. She didn't want to take the trail by the lake, then or ever.

When they were near the clearing, Janna stopped so suddenly that Kyle bumped into her from behind.

"What's the matter, Janna?"

"I thought I heard something." She tried to still the thumping of her heart, to *hear*. There was nothing, no sound, though the shadows shifted in her mind once more. "I guess it wasn't—"

This time there was no mistake about it. Karen's voice shouting, drifting between the trees. Wordless and meaningless, it shivered against her nerves.

"Come on," Kyle said. She hardly needed the urging. Forgetting the slick footing, Janna ran.

The lake lay like a sheet of pitted steel under the

slow hammering of the rain. Janna slid to a stop at the edge of the woods, catching her breath. Kyle moved past her and stopped as well.

"I don't see her. Would she have gone on toward home?"

Janna shook her head. "I don't think she'd leave here, not willingly." Her eyes went automatically to Karen's totem. "I always have to pry her away from that."

Its exposed face gleamed wetly under the gray clouds, showing odd diffused highlights. One hollow eye, turned up to the sky, was half-filled with water. A pair of yellowed needles floated there, jumping wildly whenever a drop hit their tiny puddle. A trickle of water ran through the deep lines incising a paw, only partly uncovered above the eye. The powdery debris of years of decay was washing away and with it the weight of age. The totem looked newer. And there was no sign, anywhere, of Karen.

"Hey, I don't blame her. It's fantastic. I always thought it was just an old mossy log. Mark will want to know about this." Kyle's eyes left the totem, scanning the ground. "Nobody else has been here, as far as I can tell. I'm not even sure which way she went."

"Do you think maybe she's gotten lost?" Janna turned slowly, searching for some indication of her sister's presence, unable to accept the deserted scene. Karen had been shouting; maybe she was in trouble. Where *was* she?

"Could be," Kyle said, but Janna didn't miss his glance at the water. Janna was afraid even to think in that direction. She drew a deep breath to shout herself but couldn't force any sound out of her throat.

When it finally came, the voice startled her. "Wait! Please wait!" Urgent, almost directionless, the cry rang across the clearing and was absorbed without an echo by the trees.

Kyle pointed across the narrow beach toward the rising hill, where the trees crowded the shore and the ridge dropped almost straight into the water. "Over there, I think."

Her sister's figure looked so tiny that Janna almost missed the movement between the trunks. Karen was scrambling away from them, following the curve of the shore. Each step took her higher as the bank grew steeper. As Janna watched, Karen stopped and stared across the water, calling out again. Her foot slipped in the crumbling earth, and she caught herself on a tree. Dirt and rocks pattered into the water far below as she struggled to regain her footing. Janna tensed as though even from this distance she could somehow help her sister.

"We'd better get her before she falls in," Kyle half whispered into Janna's ear. "It looks deep over there."

There was a path of sorts leading around the edge of the water, probably an old game trail. They ran for it and hurried upward, dodging thorny branches and trying to keep their footing on the rugged surface. The drop to the lake was steeper the farther they went, the water deep and heavily snagged.

A thread of tension stretched between Janna and Kyle. As soon as they had entered the trail, they lost sight of Karen in the thick growth ahead. They were going in the right general direction, but they couldn't see her. All too aware of what could happen to the smaller girl so high on that treacherous hillside, they scrambled onward.

Karen's voice reached them from time to time, sometimes seeming closer, sometimes distorted by the thick brush into seeming farther away. No real guide, it at least assured them that Karen was still all right.

"Wait!" Half scream, half sob, the cry was suddenly close ahead. Janna and Kyle broke out of the undergrowth where it ended abruptly in an open space. Only a few yards farther on, at the top of a small slide area, Karen sat on an outcrop of rock, slouching and dejected, staring ahead. Breathless, her face scratched and dirty, she kicked at a weathered splinter of the stone as she heard Janna and Kyle come up beside her. It spun out and down, into the water.

"I couldn't keep up."

"With what, Karen?" Her sister must have followed an animal up here. But the trail seemed to end at the upthrust rock formation, and brush grew thick and impenetrable beyond it. Nothing could have come through there.

"With him." Karen gestured along the curve of the hill, down near the lake's edge. "He called my name and walked away. But I couldn't keep up, and he doesn't wait."

Automatically, Janna's gaze followed Karen's. A pulsebeat's apprehension touched her as she looked and saw only a flicker of leaves in the gusting breeze and a drifting rope of mist touching the water. Then for one wild moment she caught another movement, a fading glimpse of a weathered face turning away. Hunched and indistinct, a figure pushed through the brush, and the whispering sadness surged.

HEART RACING, JANNA CLOSED HER EYES.
Logic told her she couldn't have seen anything, no hazy fading figure under the trees. Shadows moving restlessly in her own mind whispered
otherwise.

Janna opened her eyes, rejecting that silent message. Kyle was looking at her with concern, but said
nothing.

"There's no one there, Karen," she said, sup-
pressing the slight quaver in her own voice. No one,
she told herself fiercely.

"He's right there, by that tree."

Janna sighed. "Let's go." She reached for her
sister's hand, to pull her to her feet, and was left
grasping at the air when Karen jerked it away.

"You can't see him." Karen looked up at her then,
with an odd, assessing gaze. "Not either one of you.
They call him He-who-walks-between-the-worlds,
and he's wearing a brown cape of . . . of—" she
paused and tilted her head, as though she were lis-

tening. "It's woven cedar bark. . . . bark, because of the rain. And he's wearing a tall funny hat with a twisty top. It has a picture on it, of a—" Again she paused, then went on, and Janna shivered to think how much she sounded like someone repeating a whispered message. "It's a mountain goat."

"Quit it. There's nothing there."

"You just can't see him, that's all. Maybe he doesn't want you to." The wind gusted again then, a strong, sharp push of air, and the uneasiness wrapped around them from the lake. "There! Did you hear—"

The breeze died away. Karen jumped to her feet, wailing toward the far, empty shore.

"No! Come back!" For a long moment she stood tense, as though willing that figure to come again, but gradually her shoulders slumped in defeat.

Without a word, Kyle started down the hillside. Karen turned and started picking her way down toward the beach. Behind her, Janna kept her eyes on the trail, trying to shut out the water, the long drop. Brush and trees closed around them again, and she felt safer. Karen stopped once, looking back around the end of the lake, searching. She reached back and slipped one cold hand into Janna's.

When they reached the beach again, she pulled away and ran ahead to her totem pole and stood with her fingertips lightly touching the shining wood.

"You're soaked, Karen. Come on."

"I saw him, Janna."

"Sure." Karen turned reluctantly away from the lake and passed her sister and Kyle, shoulders drooping.

"Karen." Janna tried to hold back the question, but it slipped by. "Your voices—do you hear them now?"

A moment Karen paused, no more. "Don't you?" was all she said.

Janna watched in silence as she disappeared into the trees toward home, then turned at last to face Kyle's questioning eyes, as the rain dropped like a gray curtain around them.

"What was all that about this afternoon?" Kyle had held his peace as he walked her the rest of the way home. The soggy woods weren't the best place to discuss anything, especially if it would further upset Karen. When they got to the house there wasn't a minute's privacy. But Janna had known the moment would come, ever since they stood facing each other at the whispering lakeshore. What Karen saw, what Janna felt—neither had touched Kyle.

Pulling at his seemingly bottomless drink, her father, silently watching the TV, had made no comment when Kyle came back later that evening. Karen sat by his chair, quiet. She failed to respond even to Kyle. When the show ended, her father stood and took his glass into the kitchen. Coming back into the room, his face shadowed against the brighter light, he spoke with a soft slur.

"Time for bed, Karen."

Karen looked up at him, and Janna could see the change. Her little sister wanted desperately to please her father. To be forgiven.

She got up without a word and went up the stairs.

Her father followed unsteadily and paused just below the top. "Not too late, Janna."

"Sure, Dad. 'Night." He muttered a response and was gone.

Kyle had pulled Janna down to sit next to him on the couch. Now he was playing absently with her fingers, frowning down at them. "You asked Karen if she heard something. Voices."

"She says she hears them, talking to her or singing or something, in the rain." The time for hesitation was past; it felt good now to be able to tell Kyle.

"You believe her?" He was still looking down; Janna couldn't get a clue to how he felt.

"I—maybe I do." Her throat felt suddenly dry, but she forced herself to go on. "Sometimes I think that I feel something strange about that lake or that maybe I hear something, too."

Slowly, Kyle lifted his head, brought his eyes to meet hers.

"Maybe you do."

It was the last thing she had expected him to say.

"That's impossible," Janna whispered.

"Probably," he said. Kyle looked across the room at nothing. "Look, your family has been through a lot. . . . "

"So you think Karen's imagining all this because she thinks she killed Mom?"

Kyle shrugged. "I don't know what to think. I've spent enough time around Mark to keep an open mind about it. There's that totem pole Karen found, and what she said today sounded too detailed for her to be making it up. But I still think we should look for a rational explanation before we jump to the conclusion that Karen's having a paranormal experience."

Janna barely shook her head, seeing the gray sheet of water in her mind and groping after an elusive impression. "There's a feeling there, like an ancient sadness. . . . " She spoke without thinking, and her voice trailed off as Kyle's hand tightened on her own.

"Are you saying you heard something, too?"

"No—yes. I don't know!" Janna shifted uncomfortably on the couch. "How many totems do you think are there?"

"Totems," Kyle repeated. He started playing with her fingers once more, eyes down. "I thought there was only the one."

"Maybe not. Half the snags in that end of the lake are the same shape as the pole Karen found." Janna wished she knew what he was thinking, whether he was beginning to think she and Karen were crazy.

She wished she knew what she believed herself. "Could there have been a village there once?"

He pursed his lips in a soundless whistle. "I suppose anything's possible. There was a search a couple of years ago for a lost Indian village, down a little closer to the coast. I don't think they ever found it. I could ask Mark. He was involved with it."

Janna felt her heart squeeze at the thought of telling Mark about the things that had happened. She shook her head. "No, don't."

"Janna, I'm worried about your sister. Maybe he can help." When she shook her head again, Kyle went on. "This is the kind of thing Mark is especially interested in. That totem of Karen's alone would bring him running, and when you add the paranormal angle . . . " Kyle suppressed a yawn, looked at his watch, and stood up. "It's getting late. I'd better go before my mom sends for the Marines. Things are kind of tense around my place lately."

"Your dad?" He nodded, and Janna stood reluctantly. "Thanks for coming over, Kyle."

"Anytime." He kissed her lightly and opened the door. "Janna? Be careful about the lake."

"I will," she assured him.

"Okay. In the meantime, if you're sure you don't want me to talk to Mark, I'm going to borrow some of his books. I'm sure he's got something that might help us out." He looked at her seriously. "If Karen saw something at that lake today, I want to see if I can find out *why*, get some kind of clue what's happening, or at least be able to decide it's all in her mind."

"And then?" Janna felt a chill and knew it wasn't from the cold air swirling through the doorway. Discussing it was giving the whole episode more reality than she wanted to grant it.

He shrugged. "And then, I don't know. Just be careful."

She closed the door slowly behind him.

Dad's light was still on when she passed his room. She stood for a moment inside the door of her own room, listening for movement from Karen's bed. Nothing. Certain her sister was asleep, Janna undressed without a light and slid silently under the covers.

"Janna?" Karen asked suddenly. "Where do people go when they die?"

Without warning the question slapped at Janna. Time blinked, she thought, and someone died, and they were gone. As easily as a candle flame taken by the wind. They moved away to the satin side of the casket lid and the dark cool side of the grass. They left without saying good-bye. In a breath they moved from now to yesterday, and maybe that was all—forever. Impossible to say that now to Karen.

"Where, Janna?" Springs creaked in the other bed as Karen sat up.

"I don't know," Janna whispered at last. She'd asked herself the same question enough times and still had no answer, for herself or anyone else. Least of all for Karen. "Just away. Far away."

"Everybody?" Karen persisted.

"I guess. They can't just—hang around." She stretched out under the covers, absorbing the shock of the cold sheets against her skin. "Go to sleep."

Still Karen sat, a solid motionless lump in the deep dark at the head of her bed. The feeble light creeping under the door from Dad's room reached only as far as her upraised knees, glimmering faintly on the quilt. "Does everyone go to the same place?"

"No, I don't suppose they do. You know, all that stuff about heaven and hell. Is that what you mean?"

Karen didn't answer.

"What if someone didn't go? What if they just stayed in the same place?"

"I don't know. That's what a ghost would be, I guess," Janna said. She stiffened, hearing her own words. A ghost. For just a moment she saw again a dark face with secret eyes, turning. Then the vision ran together and changed, and it was her mother's face, turning, and gone. "Mom's dead, Karen. She's just—gone," Janna whispered at last.

Karen's voice was small, barely audible. "I know."

8

THERE WAS NO ONE HERE.

Janna stood next to Karen, beside the fallen totem, and looked around the clearing. A few scattered drops leaked from the clouds, but that was all. The lake was almost motionless.

Had she really expected someone—some*thing?*—to be here? Janna couldn't explain, even to herself, the pull she had felt bringing her here today. Once again she had allowed Karen's persistence to win out on the way home from school. Perhaps it was fear that Karen would find a way to come here alone. But Janna had found herself, oddly, half wanting, half fearing to come, too. Now all she felt was a curious disappointment.

As she stood by the lake, the shadows in Janna's mind were silent. Only her own memories, her own troubled dreams of faces that turned away and melted into darkness, lay inside her head. The presence she had sensed before, that had made her unable to dismiss entirely Karen's claims of voices and visions, was gone from the lake.

76

Then a sudden flutter of movement atop the tallest of the standing totems caught her eye. The owl was there again, launching itself into the air toward them. Silent white wings stroked the wind, and the owl drifted down to land on Karen's totem. Black talons bit into the wood, then relaxed. Unalarmed by their presence, the bird folded its wings and hunched itself comfortably, watching Karen with great yellow eyes. There was something unnatural in its calm, and Janna felt a ripple of unease.

Karen glanced at the bird, then resumed picking the crumbling moss from the carvings. The paw was fully exposed now, grasping with wicked claws at the forehead of the figure below. Janna wasn't entirely sure she wanted to know what kind of creature it belonged to.

Opening its hooked black beak, the owl breathed out a low chirring sound, leaning forward. Karen looked up, meeting the burning golden eyes, and nodded slightly. Then she went back to working at the moss, and the bird seemed intent on her progress. It sidled closer, dipping its head to poke delicately at the spongy green growth, chirring again. Janna found the bird's presence, its closeness to her sister, disturbing.

"We have to go, Karen."

"The Guardian wants me to finish," Karen said. She pulled away a long green strip and dropped it to the ground, watching the owl. "It belongs to *him*."

"What do you mean 'Guardian'? It's just an old

77

owl. Come on, I've got homework to do." Janna wouldn't think about that walking memory, the hunched figure that turned and faded into another world.

"It's the Guardian," Karen repeated stubbornly. "It knows my name."

Janna's unease crystalized suddenly into irritation, and she scooped up a fir cone to throw at the bird. She only meant to frighten it into flight, and the cone bounced harmlessly against the totem beside its feet. Talons tightened convulsively, piercing the rotting cedar, the wings stirred and settled. Slowly then, the feathered head swiveled until the strange, bright eyes were staring into her own.

Shock tingled through Janna and held her immobile. Round and depthless in the cruel face, the eyes were intelligent, knowing. The strength of that gaze pushed Janna back a step.

And then the owl opened its beak and cried.

The sound hung in the air, weaving and layering upon itself as the bird called again and again. Numbness gripped Janna. The first consonant was breathy and slurred, but the name was unmistakable.

Karen, Karen. The owl sat nearly motionless, calling with a relentless sadness that stirred the dark buried deep in Janna's mind. Karen.

"No," Janna whispered, rejecting the implication. The owl's voice went on and on, and suddenly she could stand it no more.

"Stop it!" she shouted. Stepping forward, Janna

78

swung blindly in the direction of the bird. Her fingers brushed something downy and cool, and then white fire slashed through her hand. She jerked it back, staring. For a frozen moment she saw a wet gleam of red edging the black beak, before powerful wings carried the bird out of reach. One last time Karen's name floated down to them, and the owl disappeared into the ringing evergreens.

"*He* knew my name, too," Karen said quietly. "All of them do. They know I didn't mean to hurt anybody."

"You didn't, Kare." Sudden tears blinded Janna's eyes, and she pulled her sister close, her aching hand forgotten. "You didn't hurt her."

Karen's body was stiff and unresponding in her arms, her eyes on the frozen face of the totem pole.

"Let's go home now, Janna. I'm tired." She pushed away, and walked into the woods. Warmth and wetness spread across the back of Janna's hand, and she stared down at it, dazed. Slow blood welled from the cut, blazing a wandering path across her skin and dripping to the ground.

Janna was still upset when she burst into the house, still shaken and scared. The blood on her hand had dried to a sticky smear, already pulling tight and cracking at the edges. The car was in the yard, but Dad was nowhere in sight. Karen had run up to their room, and Janna hesitated in the quiet before calling, "Dad?"

"Kitchen, JJ," he called back. She found him sitting at the table, surrounded by papers. Bank statement, checkbook, three days' want ads.

"Hi, Dad." On impulse she laid her face against his shoulder, grateful for the warmth and solid comfort of him, but noting automatically the slight sweetish touch of bourbon on his breath. He was sorting the papers slowly, with exaggerated care. Not really drunk, Janna thought, just hung over. Not quite cold sober, either, but maybe he'd listen.

Janna couldn't find the words to start. They used to tell him everything, she and Karen. But now . . . She sighed, straightened, and slid her books onto the table with his scattered papers. That was forever ago. Instead she went to rummage in the junk drawer for a box of Band-Aids, asking, "Is it getting bad?"

"Is what . . . ? Oh, this." He flicked the bank statement with one finger. "There's plenty. Just got to thinking, that's all. We can't live on what we have indefinitely."

"No, we can't," Janna agreed. Play the game, she thought, and pulled one of the newspapers toward her. Her finger left a dark smudge where she pressed it to the paper. "This one looks good."

He peered at the print above her finger. "Must have missed that one. Here, mark it." He looked from the paper to her hand, frowning. "That looks bad. Maybe we'd better get a couple of stitches in it. What did you do, anyway?"

"I just had an accident. I'll be all right." Janna went to rinse her hand under the tap, sucking in her breath sharply as the water penetrated the cut. It wasn't too bad, really. The owl's beak had torn the skin cleanly and had gone no deeper. Janna dabbed at it with a piece of gauze.

Her father pushed away from the table and stood up, stretching. His eyes were tired, and Janna could see the unguarded grief written there, before his barriers rose once more. "School go okay?"

"Fine." Now. She had to bring it up now or lose the chance. "You have to talk to Karen, Dad."

"She having trouble at school?"

"No, it's not that. It's that lake. That's all she can think about."

"Sounds normal enough to me." He crossed into the living room and sat down in his chair. "Something like that would be pretty exciting to a kid her age."

Janna followed, the gauze pressed to her wound. "She's still worrying about Mom. Karen asked me where she'd gone last night." He didn't answer. It was like talking to a stone wall, but Janna went on. "I think she hopes Mom's waiting somewhere. I wish you'd talk to her," she said again.

"She's all right." Barely glancing at Janna, he reached down for the *TV Guide*.

"You keep saying that! Are you so sure? Are you?" Her hands balled into a fist in her anger, and the gauze began to redden. Her voice sounded tired, even to her own ears. "She needs your help, Dad."

"My help? Lot of good that would do her." His foot brushed aside the glass that had fallen from his hand the night before, by accident maybe. "I can't even help myself."

Karen disappeared on Sunday.

Lunch was ready. Janna pulled half a leftover casserole out of the oven and carried it to the table to cool a minute, then looked into the living room.

"Karen, tell Dad it's time to eat, okay? I've got to finish setting the table." Karen got up from the old movie she was watching and shrugged into her coat as Janna turned back toward the kitchen. "He's out in the garage," she added. The door closed loudly behind her little sister.

Fifteen minutes later Karen still hadn't returned. Muttering to herself, Janna dodged through the rain and poked her head inside the garage door.

"Hey you guys, it's getting cold."

Her dad dropped a rusted chain onto a pile of junk and flexed his hands. He was alone. "Lunch ready?"

Janna nodded, pushing away a finger of worry. "I sent Karen to tell you almost twenty minutes ago."

He shook his head, following her out and closing the door. "Haven't seen her. You sure she left the house?"

"I heard her go."

82

Both of them turned toward the drive, the beginning of the trail. And knowledge looked back at Janna out of her father's eyes. The lake.

"You go back inside before you freeze. I'll get her," Dad said. "Already got my coat and boots on anyway. I want to see what's so fascinating about the lake."

Minutes passed slowly. Janna fidgeted around the kitchen, putting the casserole back into the oven, straightening a place setting. Her eyes kept going to the clock. Twenty minutes. Thirty minutes. Maybe Karen hadn't gone there. She might have fallen, hurt herself.

Or she might have followed someone, something, that called her name, and faded away. Janna pushed the thought out of her mind, refusing even to think of it.

Footsteps on the wooden front porch. Janna started as Karen burst into the living room and ran upstairs, shoulders slumped and face blotchy with crying. Their father closed the door, his face unusually stern and pale. He stopped to hang up his coat before coming into the kitchen. Matted with damp, the hair clung close to his head, and his fingers were red with cold.

Janna poured a cup of coffee and placed it on the table for him. He sank down into a chair and cupped his hands around the steaming mug. A long minute he stared down into it before meeting her gaze. There was an unsettled look in his eyes.

83

"Where did you find her, Dad?"

"At the lake. She was balanced on the very end of that carved log you told me about. Leaning out, stirring the water with a stick, of all the harebrained things." He took a cautious sip, set the cup down again. A trickle of water ran down in front of his ear. He didn't seem to feel it. "Janna, that lake is so full of snags that if she fell in she might never come up. We'd never know what happened to her."

"I know. I've tried to tell her, but she just says she can swim well enough."

He snorted. "Swimming has nothing to do with it. Anyway, I've told her to stay away from there. Think that'll stop her going off again?" He looked uncertainly up at Janna. The crisis over, he was already retreating back into his haze, already pushing it back onto her.

She brought her own cup to the table and took a seat next to him.

"Dad." Her voice was tight with the receding edges of fear. Karen was safe. This time. But what about the next time? The fear would be back. It would always be back. "Karen thinks there's something there, waiting. Calling in the rain for Karen to come. That's why she ran away."

"Oh come on, Janna!" He scowled in exasperation. "Your sister's playing some kind of game. There's nothing there. What's the matter with you?"

"Karen believes it, Dad. I've been with her when she's said she's heard or seen things. Kyle and I

84

almost lost her when she wandered off, supposedly following someone or something. What does she have to do, walk into that lake, before you'll believe me?" He didn't answer, just looked away and sipped at his coffee. "Didn't you notice anything strange there, Dad? A funny feeling or anything?"

It was the wrong question.

"Like out of a bottle, eh?" He gave her an odd glance from the corner of his eyes. "If you're looking for some evidence that I drink too much, you're out there. No d.t.'s, no hallucinations, nothing. I keep telling you there's nothing wrong with me."

"Dad, it's not—" Janna began.

He stood up and stalked from the room. "Mind your own business, Janna."

An hour later he went out.

Janna stood at the window and watched as the rain spattered the glass and drowned the wind, dissolving the hours and soaking them into the greedy earth.

That was the night Karen began humming.

It was the night the shadows came to the house.

JANNA WENT TO BED EARLY, HEAVY-eyed and weary, and found that she couldn't sleep. Her hand still ached where the owl had slashed it, and she tried not to remember that hollow voice crying her sister's name to the sky. She tossed on her bed and closed her ears to the pattering of the rain. In her mind she played over the passages of the flute solo she was working on for the concert, but it didn't help. The rain wove its pattern around and through her brain, distorting the rhythms, altering the melody.

The rain was the key, she thought. Karen seemed normal enough, until the rain disturbed the water, perhaps waking something, freeing it to reach out. . . . Restlessly, Janna turned away from the thought.

Some quality of the air told her that it was well into the small hours of the morning when her dad came home. He gunned the engine of the car before shutting it off and crashed into a chair on his unsteady way toward the stairs. Janna pretended to be asleep when he looked into their room. A few minutes later she heard him fall heavily into bed, and the quiet returned.

And in the quiet the shadows came. They peopled the darkness so softly that Janna never knew quite when they had come.

The night had grown heavy, and Janna slipped into a state between waking and sleep. The sound of her sister's easy breathing melded with the sliding raindrops, and a flicker of dream fragments painted the darkness. The rustle of coarse cloth hovered on the edge of her awareness and faded away.

Karen's voice reached through the thick air, pulling Janna abruptly away from the edge of sleep. She found herself sitting up, groggy and disoriented, heart pounding.

Karen was humming.

The melody was an eerie thread of sound, lacing the night with a pattern of grief. Minor keys and unconventional intervals made the song haunting, weighted with distilled heartbreak. And old, somehow, old and alien.

It went on and on, the same few notes again and again, and Janna sat transfixed, barely breathing. In the deep of the night, she felt the familiarity of the music, like a message, something she had to understand. And then a clear memory: Karen standing in the lisping rain, saying, "They're singing."

She had grabbed Karen and run then, closing her mind to the thought that she had heard it too. Now, the same eerie notes whispered out of the darkness of her own room, and there was nowhere to run.

As Karen continued to hum, Janna thought she saw shadows shift in the corners, rustling out of the inky black. Something was there. Janna knew suddenly with a sense she couldn't identify that the room was crowded, that around her pressed the sad shadows of others long gone. She could feel the cold earth that sucked at their bones with greedy hunger, the falling rain that merged their remaining substance with the soil beneath, eating away the ties that bound them.

Karen hummed her broken, repeated snatch of song, weaving world to world, and voices unheard chanted with her. Janna wanted to move, to break the unnatural stillness, and she couldn't. She could only feel the images, and know the lost aching of ones almost past hope.

It was Karen who finally broke the spell. Her voice faltered, drifted into nothing, and on the same note silence fell among the shadows. Wiggling, she turned her cheek to the pillow and sighed. Out of the dark at the head of her bed came a murmured benediction and a soft clicking like pebbles swaying on threads in the wind, weak and far off. Janna felt a hunched figure turning away.

The room was empty.

Her mind was clear once more, only her own memories remaining. Her sister slept peacefully, unaware that she had served as a conductor, a channel for a grief Janna could only guess at. Her own seemed pale in comparison.

Relaxing fingers that clutched painfully at the quilt, Janna lay back down and tried to control her shivering. No harm had come to them, but still she felt numb with fear.

The strange liquid tune, so unbearably sad, hung in her mind until she slept.

The next day seemed to go on forever. Kyle asked Janna what was the matter, and frowned at her distracted answer. Even Mark Nestor noticed. He called her to his desk after class.

"Janna, I just graded the test we did yesterday, and I'm concerned. You only pulled a C on it," he told her, laying the offending paper in front of him.

That finally penetrated the haze that had fogged her mind since last night. It was the lowest math grade she had ever gotten, and she had to do well in this class, to balance all the ones she was failing.

"A C?" she repeated, but made no move to examine the paper.

"Normally that wouldn't bother me; most of these benighted souls are lucky to do that well. But you're different." He was looking steadily up at her, but she refused to meet his eyes. "Now all your work seems to be going downhill."

"Yes, sir." If only he knew.

He smiled, and she felt the tug of his charm. The expression transformed his face. "Don't 'sir' me. You know better than that." His smile faded. "Kyle mentioned that you're dropping the extra credit problems. Want to tell me why?"

Her gaze fastened on the top button of his shirt. "It was just too much, I guess. I wasn't getting anywhere with them."

"Too busy ghost hunting, maybe?"

Slowly, painfully, Janna raised her eyes to meet his. She expected a look of disbelief, or maybe amusement. Instead, she could read only warm interest. Some knot inside of her began to loosen. "Kyle told you?"

He shook his head then. "Nothing, really. There was just something about all his crafty questions, and the books he was looking over. I thought maybe you could tell me a little more about it."

"It's nothing, really," Janna said quickly. "Can I go now? I need to catch up on yesterday's assignment."

The teacher sighed. "Certainly. Here." He pushed the test paper across the desk at her and leaned back, his look searching. "If you need some help, Janna, I want you to know you can call on me. Whatever it is. Okay?"

She nodded, managing a tight smile, and turned away.

★   ★   ★

"Did you get the books?" Janna asked as soon as they got off the bus.

Kyle nodded, adjusting his backpack on one shoulder. Karen had already run far ahead. "It's not easy reading. I haven't found anything yet."

"You didn't fool Mark much. He knows something is up." Skirting a soggy spot on the trail, Janna shoved her fists deep into her pockets. "Anyway, there's got to be something to help explain all this."

"Maybe." It had become a habit by now for him to walk them home. Janna appreciated his calm good sense, but now he sounded troubled. "I don't think you should put too much faith in our finding the answers in a book."

"I don't know what else we can do, Kyle." Janna felt suddenly small and helpless. "There was something in our room last night. I could feel it, almost see it. It seemed to be whispering to Karen."

Kyle stopped abruptly, catching at her hand to stop her as well. "You didn't tell me about that. It wasn't just Karen? You also felt something was really there?"

Janna nodded. "It was creepy. The room felt— crowded, somehow. As though if I could just look a little harder I'd see someone, and if I could just listen a little harder I'd hear them, too. It was scary."

"Yeah. Scary says it." Kyle let her go. "So what happened?"

"Nothing," Janna said. "Karen hummed this

weird melody in her sleep, and the air almost seemed to hum with her, and I felt—I felt like the rain outside was soaking through me and melting me away. Then Karen stopped humming, and they were gone."

Kyle whistled. "Just like that. That's all?"

"That's all." For a long moment Janna stared at him, and Kyle stared back, eyes deep and unreadable. Then together they turned and moved on. Silence as brittle as cellophane wrapped around them as they went on toward the lake.

Karen was already there, standing by her totem. The rain had nearly gone, and a fitful wind funneled off the ridges and turned the last leaves on the maples and alders so that their pale undersides flashed against the darker evergreens. The wind played across the water, touching and moving on, wrinkling and smoothing the surface at a whim. Karen's hair ruffled in the breeze, parting over one ear and whipping into her eyes.

Hands in pockets, unmoving, she gave no sign that she had heard Janna and Kyle arrive. She simply stood, and then she started to hum again, the odd broken rhythms and harmonies eddying in the air. The white owl was perched on top of the tallest totem, staring at her with a stony intensity. Karen hummed, and on the edge of reality Janna thought she heard other voices that chanted so softly that at times they were lost beneath the sound of wind in the branches.

92

A tightness inside Janna's head shrilled a warning, and she turned to Kyle.

"Something's happening," she said urgently. "Help me get Karen—"

And then, as one voice, the chanting seemed to stop, and Janna felt more than heard a rattle shaken, commanding and authoritative. The sudden silence was a vacuum, waiting.

Faltering slightly, Karen began to sing. She sounded older, her voice roughened by despair and an ageless loneliness. Janna stood transfixed, frozen by the weight of wanting in her sister's voice, in the words she couldn't understand. For a long moment she could only stand there, aware of her own heart hammering, of the spinning leaves and the rags of cloud blowing away from the high ridges. Her mind seemed full of the keening whisper she could not quite hear, of huddled faceless figures she could not quite see. A part of her wanted to scream.

"Janna? What is it?" Kyle grasped her shoulder, shaking her slightly, and the foggy wrapping in her mind began to shred.

"No." Her voice came out as a dry whisper, easily drowned by the melody. Not enough to reach Karen, on the other side of the song. Kyle's fingers tightened, jabbing painfully into muscles hard with tension, and then Janna did cry out. "No!"

Karen stopped in midphrase. The breathless silence seemed as loud as the shout, echoing, running thin, ending. "No?" Karen repeated.

With a sense of shifting focus that was sharp and dizzying, a curtain of normality dropped around them again.

"Are you all right?" Kyle's tone was strained and low, close beside her ear.

Janna nodded, numb. The clearing was still and ordinary, empty once more but for them. There might never have been a strange compelling song, a panicked shout. Slowly, she began to relax.

"Did I get it wrong?" Karen's question was flat and unemotional.

Janna whirled to face her sister, slipping slightly in the mud, and her breath caught painfully. Karen stood oddly immobile, dreamer in a dream, unfocused eyes wide and staring. The sight hit Janna like ice creeping along her nerves, the touch of lake water on her skin.

"You told me to sing the sky bridge." Karen's gaze went through Janna and beyond, to where the white owl waited, unmoving. "Wasn't it right?"

"Karen? Karen, wake up!" There was a shrill edge of panic in Janna's voice, and it must have penetrated her sister's daze. Karen looked slowly around, blinking.

"Did you say something, Janna?"

"Yes." The tension inside of her snapped, and she felt suddenly limp. "It's time to go home."

"Okay" was all Karen said, turning her back casually on the gray water and walking away.

Kyle's hands were still tight on Janna's shoulder.

He turned her to face him, and his eyes were worried.

"Was that what Karen sang last night?"

The last of the numbness dissolved then, and Janna leaned her head on his chest and began to shake. He put his arms around her.

"She didn't know the words last night. Just the melody."

"I don't like this, Janna." Kyle looked past her, to where the owl waited silently on its totem. "I don't feel what you both seem to feel, but something is definitely weird. If something really is happening here and Karen's part of it, it could be dangerous."

"I know." Janna swallowed past the ache in her throat. "What can we *do*?"

He sighed. "I don't know, but we're not going to find the answer in a book. I think it's time we talked to Mark. As you said, he already knows something strange is going on. If he doesn't know what to do, maybe he'll be able to tell us who does."

10

THE BURRING NOISE OF A DISTANT phone echoed through the wire. Janna clutched the cord, her ear pressed to the back of the receiver that Kyle held to his head. On and on the phone rang, no one answering. At last he dropped the phone back onto its cradle.

"Mark must have gone out. We'll have to try again later." He pushed one hand through his wet hair, looking gravely at Janna. Upstairs the floor creaked as Karen walked across the room and flopped onto her bed. "I don't know, maybe I *did* feel something strange at the lake, too."

"It was like there was someone there, just out of sight. The same as last night, in our room."

"You think the lake is haunted?"

"I—" Janna hesitated, feeling a stir of inexplicable pity. "Yes. And they've been hurt by something. I want to help them."

"*Help* them?" Kyle exploded. "Janna, are you crazy?"

She looked up to meet his eyes and shook her head slowly. "I don't think so. But I feel some of what they feel. Some of the pain," she whispered.

"We'll end it, then. For you, anyway. There's got to be something we can do." He placed his hands on her shoulders, and the pressure woke an ache where his fingers had dug into her earlier. "Janna, how much of it is your own grief, do you think? You have to come to terms with that. No matter what we do, your mother will still be dead."

She looked away, throat suddenly chokingly tight. "Maybe it should have been me. It would be easier—"

His hands dropped from her as though she had become too hot to touch.

"Grow up, Janna." He stepped back from her. "You're not that much different from Karen or your dad. It's easier to blame yourself than to put it behind you and go on living. Don't you think if you stopped filling in for your mother, your dad'd have to wake up a little?"

She was silent a long time. The world would fall apart, maybe, if she didn't fill in for Mom. In misery, Janna admitted to herself that the world had fallen apart anyway. And in a sudden caustic tide, there was anger. Janna resisted it for a minute, then let it flood through her.

"What do you know about it? At least your family is intact!" she flared, and immediately regretted it.

"Yeah, it's intact." Kyle's mouth twisted bitterly. "Sometimes that's not all it's cracked up to be, either."

"Kyle, I'm sorry—" she began.

"Forget it," he said gruffly, turning away and yanking the door open. Gray twilight seeped into the room. "If Mark can't help us, he'll know who can. I'm going to keep calling until I get an answer."

She stood there, unable to reply, and after a moment he went out and shut the door. Janna rushed to the window, watching him fade into the gathering gloom, hunched against the damp and the hurt. She almost called him back. Almost.

Long after Karen had gone to bed, Janna sat alone in the living room. Their father had gone out just after dinner, and in the silence she could no longer keep her fears at bay.

What if, at the lake, something waited between life and afterlife? Karen certainly believed it, and Janna, too, had felt a sense of grief that lay heavy there, festering below the surface, reaching out. . . . Whatever it was seemed to touch Karen, who was vulnerable and reaching out in her own pain. It touched her and resonated within her and perhaps was magnified.

What could she do? Dad was out. He'd blocked her away neatly with his certainty it was all imagination, or another attempt to get at him.

Kyle was right—there was nowhere to turn but to Mark.

It was a long walk out to the road the next morning. Karen seemed willing to pass by the trail, until a breeze rose up from nowhere and tugged at their hair. It shifted about, grabbing a few of the last faded leaves to fling them at Janna and Karen, pushing hard at the branches that lined the road. Without warning it reversed itself, doubling around them, blowing from the ridges with a cold thread of silent music before it died, leaving nothing but the tingle of fear.

"We'll take the lane from now on," Janna said quickly. She had to force the words past a sudden dryness in her throat.

Karen was backing away down the lane. "You can't keep me away," she said with ominous quiet. "I have to go there. I have to."

The same wind had wrapped around her, too. Neither of them said another word all the way out to the road.

Kyle boarded the bus unusually subdued, carrying a bulging gym bag. He was huddled down into his collar, and when he sat next to Janna he kept his face turned slightly away.

Janna took a deep breath and stuttered out the words of apology.

"I'm sorry about last night, Kyle. You were right."

He slouched deeper into the seat. "S'okay."

"No it isn't. You were right about a lot of things." There was an awkward pause. Kyle said nothing. "Did you talk to Mark?"

"Tried to. He didn't answer." Still Kyle hadn't looked at her.

"Are you all right?" Janna asked, suddenly concerned. "Look at me, please."

"I'm okay," he muttered, but at last he turned toward her. Janna caught her breath then, understanding why he'd hidden in his coat collar. A dark bruise, puffed and ugly, marred his cheekbone. He gave her a half smile. "Pretty, isn't it?"

It was horrible, swelling there on his face. Even his eye was half-closed. "Your dad?"

Kyle nodded. Now that his face was uncovered, he folded his collar back down out of the way. "Grant's Logging laid off a couple of crews yesterday, so he's out of work again. Nothing new."

"What will you do?" It came out as little more than a whisper, as her eyes kept going back to the vivid bruise.

"Stay out of his way until he gets on somewhere else, I guess." His shrug was eloquent. "Go to Mark's, probably. Don't make a big deal about it, Janna."

Silence fell between them again and Janna fidgeted, staring out the window. When she craned her neck to look up past the trees, gray drops of rain slanted toward her eyes, only to veer off and resume their straight fall behind her. The bus grew more crowded.

Kyle reached out and took her hand in his own. "I worried about you all night. While my folks screamed at each other, all I could think about was you, not myself. That's a first."

She hadn't realized how much it meant to her, knowing Kyle lived so close, until now when she knew he might not come home today. Janna didn't know what to say, so she just returned the pressure of his hand.

It wasn't until the beginning of lunch that they were able to make their way to Mark's room. Kyle pushed the door open ahead of her and stopped so suddenly that Janna ran into him.

A woman's voice said, "May I help you?"

Janna peered around Kyle's suddenly still form. Hands full of papers, a stranger sat at Mark's desk. She smiled uncertainly up at them.

"Mr. Nestor is out of town today. Is there something I can help you with?"

11

DAD WAS GONE AND THERE WAS A NOTE
on the table when Janna got home. She read it
quickly, crumpled it in sudden anger, and tossed it
into the garbage. He'd gone into town, no need to
say where. Janna knew, and she was tired of worrying about it. Let him take his own risks. He was
an adult.

Absently, Janna laid her books on the table, wishing Kyle were there. He had gone to Mark's home
after school, promising to call as soon as Mark returned. There was nothing she could do but wait.

"I can't find my red crayon." Karen stood in the
doorway, frowning. Luckily, Karen had followed
Janna up the lane from the bus and had not insisted
on the trail. "I need my red crayon, Janna. I *really*
need it."

Janna shuffled through her papers, looking for her
assignment. She wasn't very interested in the crayon.
"It might have gotten thrown in the junk drawer if
you left it out."

Karen rummaged around for a minute and left,

unsatisfied. Sounds of searching came from upstairs. Janna sighed and began scrubbing some potatoes for dinner. At least Karen was acting like a normal kid for the time being. The potatoes in the oven, Janna sat down with her homework and soon forgot everything else.

Finished at last, Janna pushed her homework away. She stretched and glanced up at the clock, then, startled, at the window. The glass was a black, reflective square, spattered with rain. It was late, and dinner only half prepared. Janna jumped up and crossed the room.

Searching in the fridge for vegetables, she stopped suddenly, stiffening as a thought tickled her consciousness. One hand on the open door, she felt the cold air flow around her feet, and the silence strained at her ears. Karen. Her sister hadn't been down since she came looking for her crayons just after school, not for a snack or to use the bathroom or anything. Quietly, softly, Janna swung the refrigerator door shut.

She had a terrible feeling she was alone in the house.

The living room was a gloomy cavern, its darkness relieved only by the light that spilled from the kitchen. The upstairs was dark as well. Ordinary shadows sprang back and cowered from the lights Janna flipped on as she went.

Karen must have fallen asleep. She held that thought in her mind, willing it to be true. Outside their room she paused, telling herself she didn't want to wake Karen. Gently she pushed the door open at last, and a crooked rectangle of light widened across the floor, the wall.

Both beds were empty. Nothing moved but her own shadow. A scatter of crayons and papers, Karen's coat and boots in a damp pile. Against the roof the rain called seductively in the night, gargling a message in the gutters. Gone, gone.

Frozen in the doorway, Janna felt the truth dripping into her like ice water. They had called her sister out into the dark. And she had done nothing to stop them.

In the far corner of the room something moved, a shifting of shadow as if a few of the silent ones lingered behind, weak as rotting wood and tired as porous bones. Janna took a small step into the room.

"What have you done with her?" Her voice was gritty and dry, and when it stopped the room echoed with silence.

"What have you *done* with her?" Janna repeated, her voice rising in her fear. Around her the slippery quiet shaped itself into a sigh, and the unnatural shadows puddled together in the corner and melted away, leaving only normal dimness. The room, the entire house, felt empty. Even Janna felt empty.

Every instinct denied the feelings, the shadows. Her sister had to be hiding. . . . She ran down the hall.

Their father's room was deserted and dark, and Janna sank against the door frame. Some quality of the air told her that the room hadn't been disturbed. There was no longer any hope or excuse to hide behind. Karen was gone.

She had to force her paralyzed mind to consider what to do next. Finding Dad, waiting for him to drive out from town, would take too long.

Running to the kitchen, she dug frantically through the junk drawer, scooping things out onto the floor in her haste. It had to be here. At last her fingers closed around the flashlight, and she pulled it out. Janna thumbed the switch as she struggled into her still-wet jacket and threw the door open. Silver lancets of rain pierced and glinted through the light that spilled out the door.

For a long moment Janna looked uncertainly toward the hollow in the hills. What would happen if she went out there alone tonight? The thought made her skin tighten with a chill of fear.

And if she didn't go?

Karen could even now be lying still under the water, hair tangling with the grabbing twisted branches, eyes wide to an endless dark. The lake would never let her go, it would cradle her with its cold and cover her with a rotting shroud of fallen leaves, and they would never really know. The image was searing, unbearable, and somehow Janna choked it off.

Shivering inside her nearly useless jacket, she took a long look down the lane, hoping to see distant headlights glowing on the trees. Nothing. She was on her own.

Swallowing her fear, Janna plunged toward the woods.

Karen had been at the lake. A new section of the totem was uncovered, glistening wet faces staring back at her. Bits of moss and dirt and decayed wood washed toward the ground.

Janna's light sifted the darkness all around the totem, but the area was deserted. She found nothing but a trampled spot, small footprints partly filled with water.

"Karen? Are you here?"

The rain mocked her, provided her only answer. Before her the lake crouched like a living thing, giving nothing, waiting.

"Karen!" As she called again Janna gulped back the choking suffocation in her throat. There was nothing but a rustling sound close at her side, and she felt she was no longer alone. Janna spoke without turning her head, hardly daring to hope for a reply.

"Where is she?" Janna asked, and whispered voices shaped in her mind, answering and not answering.

We cannot sing, the night does not listen. The last moon starves to nothing and darkens. Cold earth is a mouth to eat us, a belly to imprison us. Call the names, the names. . . .

"Give her back to me," Janna pleaded, and the half-heard murmured chant surged wildly.

She will take us. Beyond the waiting, beyond the nothing, she will take us, she will take us. We will be life, we will be salmon spirits dancing. She will take us. . . .

"No!" Janna's voice was hoarse, thick and unwilling against that fierce triumph.

The Guardian has spoken, the name has been called. There is no turning back. . . .

She felt more than heard a restless shifting in the wet darkness all around her, the fading heavy sigh of coarse clothing in motion, and they were gone again.

Fear for her sister gripped her like an icy fist, and Janna scrambled onto the totem to peer down into the water. If Karen had already drowned . . .

The stippled surface bounced and broke the light, distorting the barkless trees and the scribbly lines of tangled branches. The beam reached weakly downward. Something moved below, like a hand beckoning, and behind her, around her, she heard the voices. The cloudy shadows became fascinating, the rain soothing in her ears and on her skin. Janna couldn't look away. Caught in a liquid web, she leaned farther out.

She felt her foot slide an inch, and it didn't seem

to matter. Nothing mattered. There was only the water, like a path downward. And beyond it a door, nearly closed, where the shadows gathered, waiting, just out of sight. They would ease the moment of separation, bring her down between the shadowed carved faces, and enfold her scarred spirit with their wanting. At the edge of awareness she felt the promises: an end to grief, an end to pain.

She will take us. The time is nearly done, the wait will not be long. Come, and dance in the land of the salmon. Breathe the blood of the land, give life for life for life. . . .

They sang in her mind, caroling out thought. Reaching out, offering what little they had to give. And Janna knew; she would go.

Her foot slipped again on the treacherous surface, tipping her forward and forcing her toward that door, and suddenly Janna felt only instinctive reaction. She was falling out of the world, and in a spasm of terror she pushed hard away from the lake. Light and darkness spun together as she fell, and then she was lying on the ground with one cheek pressed into the mud.

The whispering in the air went on and on, and the rain was like sharp fingers searching her hair, her face. Janna covered her ears and lay still, clenching her jaw to hold back the sobs rising in her throat. Her elbow throbbed where it had struck against something. The light was gone. In the dark, the sorrow in this place was like a mindless hunger, absorbing her own and giving it new substance. It beat against her, and when she could hold out no longer, Janna cried.

Burning, painful, the sobs welled up and out, aching against her ribs. In all the months since her mother's death, Janna had clamped down against the tears. All her crying had been weak and treacherous, sliding under her guard, quickly subdued. There had been nothing like this, hot and cleansing. Now, her defenses burned to nothing, Janna cried.

Her sobbing trailed away and ended at last, and she lay limp and hiccuping under a creeping lassitude. It would be so easy just to lie here, with the thick smell of earth and water all around her. The ground was theirs, it had drunk of their substance and waited now with an embrace cold and heavy as clay. Janna felt warmer. A spark of rational thought flared; the warmth was danger, she must move or die of hypothermia. Better, the silence promised, to take that way down through the water and never be alone. . . .

Karen would be alone then. The thought jolted through her like a current. Janna sat up suddenly, stiff muscles protesting, mind beginning to work once more. She hadn't seen her sister below and knew somehow that Karen hadn't gone that way. Not yet.

Now that she was sitting, Janna could see vague highlights picked out of the blackness around her. She struggled at first to make sense out of the faint orange glow. Light. Flashlight. Her knees jerked up and she scrambled to her feet in one motion.

The flashlight lay almost within reach, still on, half buried in a drift of sodden leaves. She would find her sister after all.

The light cut the crowding shadows with surgical precision, and they shrank away from its bright edge. Still Karen was nowhere to be seen. Her name was on Janna's tongue, but the words wouldn't leave her throat. The air belonged to *them*, not to her.

The flashlight hung at Janna's side as she tried to think. Where to look? Janna was paralyzed by the fear that whichever way she went might be the wrong one, that without a clue she could miss her sister in the dark.

And if she missed her, Karen might never see the light again.

Something in the glowing circle at her feet caught her eye. A single spot, a gleam of water out of place, claimed her attention. Janna stood frowning down at it a long moment before something finally fit together and she recognized it, one small footprint partially smeared by her fall.

In less than a minute she had found the next. It was half in the water, and Janna hesitated before turning the light full on it. The lake was shallow here over silted logs and boulders, and Karen could have waded out for some way in safety. Reluctantly, Janna turned her light across the water. The surface shivered and shifted constantly, but nothing else moved. She could make out the rigid forms of some of the standing totems, the more fluid shapes of drowned trees. Nothing else. Karen wasn't there.

Three more footprints, widely spaced, marked where Karen had stepped in especially soft ground. They led away from both road and house toward the steep trail around the lake. Janna followed beside them.

Movement, caught from the corner of her eye, arrested Janna's motion. A bending figure, a blacker blackness, the pale blur of a face turning away. And a soft skirl of clicking sounds, fading. She jerked the light around to the spot.

The figure was gone.

Weaving branches, a shiny wet barricade of growth, caught the brightness. Nothing moved but the slow nodding of the last dying leaves. The circle of light touched the branches, and in the dimness below was something else. Hardly daring to breathe, Janna brought the flash slowly down.

Karen sat huddled on the ground, unblinking in the yellow beam.

"Karen. Thank God," Janna whispered, and stepped forward. Her sister remained motionless, a sculpture carved and polished by the rain, hair and skin and clothing throwing back a wet gleam like glazed porcelain. Her head was cocked to one side, as though she listened to someone who whispered in her ear, and her eyes appeared unseeing. Janna nervously searched the brush again, but they were alone. She thought she heard the soft voice of an owl, nothing more.

Heart pounding, she covered the few paces between them and went on one knee beside the younger girl.

"Karen? It's me, baby. Wake up." There was no response, no movement. Janna reached out and tentatively touched the white face, dreading to find it cold and stiff. Her fingertips registered coolness, and the softness of life. Karen's eyes shifted then, abandoning her private visions to meet Janna's with a faraway spark of recognition.

"Mamma's coming," Karen whispered dreamily, and the words cut dark canyons in Janna's mind.

12

JANNA TOOK A DEEP BREATH AND brought both hands to Karen's shoulders, holding the flashlight in an awkward grip. The world was unreal and disjointed, set against the hushed background conversation between the rain and the lake. The light's beam danced a crazy pattern in the air as she shook her sister gently.

"Mom's dead, Karen. Remember?"

"I remember," Karen said, her eyes shifting to look beyond Janna's shoulder once more. "It was my fault. But *he* said I can see Mamma if I help."

"Dead is forever, Karen," she said softly. "Mom's gone, and it wasn't your fault."

Karen pushed weakly at her arms. "Go away, Janna. I can't hear."

"I'm taking you home." There was no response, and Janna felt a cold knot of fear for her sister tighten inside her. She gathered up the small figure and staggered to her feet. "Put your arms around my neck."

"It's almost time." Karen's voice had gone dis-

113

tant, as though something separated her from the world.

"Come on, grab hold," Janna said as calmly as she could. "There's nothing you can do for them."

"*He* was telling me what to do. He said I could see Mamma."

Janna settled her sister awkwardly and looked toward the trail. Her mouth went dry.

She felt rather than saw them. They were all around, mute, faceless forms thickening the natural darkness. They stood silent, waiting in grim patience, just beyond sight, and Janna felt her nerve begin to break. To go home, she would have to walk through that circle of death.

Karen's face dropped against Janna's shoulder and she began to cry, whispering, "I want Mamma."

They couldn't stay here. Janna swallowed nervously, facing the wall of drowned shadows. Their silence was more unnerving than their elusive whispering had been. Gripping Karen more tightly, Janna moved forward and walked among them.

She was afraid they would try to stop her, try to take her sister somehow. Instead they dissolved like smoke around her. Janna felt nothing but a strange coldness in the rain that melted against her skin, and then she knew they were gone. Behind her the clattering sound touched the air once more. She didn't look back.

She lost all sense of time as they fumbled through the woods. Her life narrowed to the step ahead and her sister. She carried Karen until her arms were afire and the lake was well behind them, then walked behind her and carried her by turns. And always Karen tried to go back.

Staggering with fatigue, Janna was carrying her again when she felt sudden space around them. Confused, she looked up and saw the lights of the house. They had made it. Janna blinked the streaming water out of her eyes, and felt a lurching disappointment. The door stood wide to the night. Dad still hadn't come home.

She was almost beyond caring when they passed under the porch roof and the rain was gone. Inside, Janna turned to push the door shut with her foot and lost her balance as it closed. She sat down hard, trying to protect Karen with her own body. Her sister didn't stir.

It didn't seem worth the effort to get up. Every muscle ached, and the room around them was a blur. She hardly even felt the cold anymore. There was a voice, hoarse and murmuring, and it was a moment before she recognized it as her own. Janna cradled her sister more comfortably in her arms. Water trickled against her skin, dripped from her hair and clothes. Wearily, she closed her eyes and lowered her cheek to Karen's head, and slipped into the quiet inside herself.

The sound of an engine came from another world, beyond a dream, where it meant nothing. Janna heard the steady droning, the heavy splashing in the drive, the abrupt silence, and it meant nothing. Even the footsteps on the wooden porch were meaningless. Only Karen's steady breathing, the weight of her body, were real.

The door opened suddenly behind her, crashing against her back and bounding away again. It hurt, and that at last penetrated to the far place where Janna had retreated.

She jerked upright, clutching Karen, and twisted to see over her shoulder. Swearing tiredly in a low mutter, her dad edged around the door and into the room. He stopped short when he saw them.

"What in hell is going on?" Karen moved convulsively in her sleep, opened bleary eyes, and stared up at him. He came farther into the room. "You're soaked."

"Please." Janna met his black frown and whispered helplessly, "Take Karen upstairs, Dad. I couldn't go any farther."

Racking shivers were suddenly tearing through her as the cold finally reached her consciousness. It was over. Dad stood towering and frowning above her for a long moment, then bent to pick Karen up. She grabbed at his neck, eyes still wide and sleepy. "Daddy."

"I'm here, baby." He kissed her white cheek, and glared down at Janna. "Better be a good story. She's like ice." He went carefully up the stairs with Karen.

Janna hugged her knees a long minute, enduring the shivers, trying to warm herself. It was no good, and finally she pushed stiffly to her feet and went up to her room.

Karen lay in a huddle on her bed, limp and passive, while Dad fumbled with her shoes. Janna stopped in the doorway, light-headed, and he spoke without turning.

"We have to warm her up. I'll get these wet things off her, while you run a hot bath. Fill the hot water bottle, too, then change and put some coffee on."

"I could help—"

"Do what I said. Now." Karen's shoes thumped together onto the floor. "We'll talk when I get downstairs."

There was no comfort in the promise.

Mechanically, Janna gathered some dry clothes and stumbled to the bathroom, wondering vaguely how much Dad had drunk. He sounded nearly sober, and he was in a temper. Maybe not too much, then.

The coffee was hot and the burned dinner scraped away by the time Dad came down. He looked less thunderous, but not by much.

"How is she?" Janna asked quietly, pouring.

He gave her a sidelong look. "About how you'd expect, soaked like that. Be lucky if she doesn't get pneumonia." He dropped Karen's clothes into the sink. They made a wet squishing sound in the chill

117

silence his words had created. His voice was hard when he spoke again. "I thought I could trust you to take care of her."

"And I thought I could trust *you* to take care of us," Janna said bitterly, jerking around to face him. Coffee slopped across the counter, and she slammed the pot down, sucking at a burned finger and looking up at him defiantly. "Why didn't you stop her? Where were you?"

He flinched, and dropped his eyes, but not before Janna saw their desolation. He knew that she was aware of where he had been, of no use to anyone in a dim tavern. The tense silence spun out, until Dad took a cup and leaned back against the countertop, watching her. He ran a hand through his damp hair, and left it standing in disarray.

"What happened?"

"I was doing my homework in here, and she must have gone out. I didn't hear her." And she should have, Janna thought bleakly. She mopped at the spilled coffee. "I went out as soon as I missed her."

He looked down into his mug. "Where did you find her?"

"At the lake." Janna didn't want to remember, to open again the well of terror. "She was just sitting there, listening into the rain. She didn't hear me when I called, not until I found her and touched her."

His eyes came up, with a startled, wary expression. "Did she give you any explanation?"

118

"Not exactly." Janna fiddled with her cup. She knew, and Karen had known there was no need for explanation. Not with the lakeshore crowded with the whispering dead. "But Dad—her first words were, 'Mamma's coming.' "

China snicked heavily against the countertop. Janna didn't look up. The sudden deep stillness seemed unbreakable, arresting.

"Mamma's coming," he repeated at last, his voice grating. "From the dead, I suppose?"

"I don't know what she meant." They couldn't be talking about Mom. The conversation was unreal, a dream within the larger nightmare. "But there is . . . something . . . there. Calling, promising. Karen said they told her she could talk to Mom. I heard them, Dad. I saw them."

"You saw—damn it, Janna, are you crazy? Don't encourage Karen in this. I mean that." His voice was low and taut with anger.

"I know. I told her—I told her Mom was dead." Janna felt cold again. "She still thinks she killed Mom. And she thinks she can find her out there— at the lake."

A low sound escaped her father, a painful breath scraped from his throat. Janna didn't dare look at him, afraid she'd see something she couldn't bear, and missed the explosive burst of motion that left his cup shattered against the base of the far wall. She wished she had missed as well hearing his dry whisper, "She's dead," and seeing the mingled anger

119

and pain on his face as he spun and strode out of the room.

Janna slumped into a chair, drained. Slowly, she put her forehead into her cupped hands and closed her eyes. Karen. Everything came back to Karen. It was Karen who suffered most from their mother's death, their father's neglect. And now it was Karen who was touched by those others, whoever they were, reaching out from the tiny lake in the woods and turning guilt and pain like a key.

What could she do? Kyle had not called. Did that mean Mark had not returned? Or did it mean Mark had thought nothing of what Kyle told him? What could any of them do anyway? Maybe Janna could take Karen and run away to their uncle in Montana— *if* she could get any of Dad's money, and if Karen would go. Straightening again and staring at the dark window, shutting out the sound of the storm fingering the glass, she tried to think it out, to plan. Her own reflection stared back, as mute and unresponsive as her brain. There was nothing more she could do.

Whatever she did, it wouldn't be enough.

The clouds broke during the night, and a thin patina of early sunlight streaked the window when Janna woke. The light banished the repelling gloom of the evergreens, and seemed to loosen the ties that bound Karen so tightly to her lake.

Janna's dizzy relief lasted just until she glanced across the room to Karen's bed.

Her sister looked small and ill, and Janna clenched her mind against the memory of the fragile porcelain Karen on the lake shore. Getting up and touching her lightly, Janna frowned. She expected fever. Instead, Karen seemed cool and lay huddled as if there weren't enough warmth under the covers. Clearly, there was no question of her going to school.

Janna took a quilt from her own bed to put over her sister, trying to warm her a little. The room was cold, and Janna shivered into her clothes, glancing at the window as she straightened her collar. Her hands froze, dropping slowly, and something inside of her curdled into a lump of fear.

The last moon starves and darkens. . . . It was a whisper in her mind, an echo from the fold in the hills. *The last moon* . . .

In the distance she saw the treetops gnawing at the tip of an emaciated sliver of white moon. Even as she watched, it dipped farther, inching away after the night. It would creep into the sky again even narrower, a pale measure of time.

The time is nearly done. . . . When the moon darkened, would the last ties that bound the shadows crumble? They would be gone, then. It would be over. If she could hold Karen just a few more days . . .

It would never be over.

Slowly Janna began to understand, fitting together the things she had heard, had felt. For some reason, whoever they were they needed Karen, to take them through that dark door she had sensed. Before it closed, and left the spirits adrift in the nothing between the worlds, where the darkness would eat their souls and leave only empty shadows of souls, howling at the gates of the world.

She remembered the intensity of their wanting, and she knew. The next few days would be the worst yet.

She was torn. Karen didn't seem seriously ill, but it was clear she would have to be carefully watched. Left alone, she would go back to the water, to sit and listen, and perhaps go through a doorway with no returning. Janna knew she should stay with Karen—yet she had to see Kyle, had to try to find some solution. She finished dressing and tapped on her dad's door as she went in.

"Dad." She shook him hard, and he pulled away, rolling over to present one shoulder to her. Janna shook him again.

"What?" he muttered.

"Karen's sick."

He sat up, groggy and unfocused, and made a futile swipe at his hair. "She very bad off?"

Janna shook her head. "No, I don't think so, but you'll have to watch her. I think she'll try to go out again."

"The kid won't be satisfied until she drowns herself, I suppose. You go ahead and go to school. I'll make sure she stays in." He swung his feet to the floor, but Janna stood hesitating, half afraid to leave Karen in his care. What if he started drinking? He looked up at her irritably. "I said to go to school. Trust me for a change, okay?"

Without a word she left the room.

13

KYLE WAS WAITING JUST INSIDE THE doors when she got to school. He dodged toward her through the crowd, and his welcoming grin drained away as he saw her worried expression.

"What's happened? Karen?"

"It's always Karen," Janna sighed, and told him about the previous night. "We need help. Did Mark—"

Kyle was looking grim. "Sorry I didn't call. He's supposed to be back this morning. The school called just before I left to confirm the time he's coming in." He took her hand and pulled her over to the wall, out of the stream of hurrying bodies. "Look, Janna, could you skip out this morning? We can't let this go any longer, and Mark will be swamped once he gets back over here. We can go to his place and wait."

"I think we're almost out of time," Janna said. "What if he can't help?"

"Then he'll know who can." He shifted his books restlessly.

She hesitated, then nodded. "Okay, let's go."

Janna stopped short, staring around in amazement when Kyle ushered her into Mark's living room.

"I told you about his collection, didn't I?" Kyle said, grinning. He prodded her forward, so he could come through the doorway and flop into a handy armchair. "This is Mark's second passion, after teaching."

"I couldn't picture it, I guess." She moved toward the nearest display, feeling strangely breathless. Some part of her knew these things. "This is wonderful."

The soft neutrals of the room provided the perfect contrast for the bold colors and designs of the Indian artwork. Built-in lighted displays held a variety of smaller objects, while most of the seating consisted of cushions on top of intricately carved bentwood boxes. Framed Indian prints in red, white, and black alternated with groupings of baskets on one wall, and from the skylighted ceiling were suspended the leering faces of cedar dancing masks. But it was the far wall, over the fireplace, that drew her most.

She crossed the room and touched the coarsely woven fabric, her finger tracing the distinctive oval eye patterns. The design was highly stylized, but Janna recognized the shape of a killer whale, enclosing its own cramped, manlike spirit. "What is this?"

Kyle came over to join her. "It's a dancing apron,

over a hundred years old. Shamans wore them during ritual dances and when they wanted extra power."

It was an odd shape, not quite rectangular, with a heavy fringe that supported dozens of dark, pointed objects. Janna brushed them idly and felt a sudden chill as they clattered gently together. She knew that sound, had heard it in the darkness of her own room. Janna backed away.

"What are they?" she whispered.

"Deer hoof rattles. Are you all right, Janna?"

She sank down onto one of the cushioned boxes, still staring at the dancing apron. Finally she dragged her gaze away, to meet his. "That sound—"

A movement in the doorway caused her to break off, turning. Janna found herself looking up into Mark's frowning face. Neither of them had heard him drive up.

"Did the school finally fall down, or are you two by any chance skipping class?" he demanded. His eyes went from her to Kyle, and his stern expression altered as he took in the livid bruise. "Another layoff?"

Kyle nodded. "I thought you wouldn't mind if I stayed here. . . . "

Mark set down the small suitcase he was carrying and stretched. "I don't, idiot, but I do mind you bringing a girl here and skipping class to do it."

"It's not like that, Mark," Kyle said quietly.

"Yeah, I know. No offense, Janna." The teacher grinned suddenly. "But I'll bet the school's still standing, so what are you doing here? It's too much to hope that you two might be studying. You'll need it, you know, for this next test."

"If that's a threat, Mark, save it." Kyle crossed the room to hand the borrowed book to Mark. The teacher took it, glanced at the title, and quirked one eyebrow.

"Interesting?"

"Very. Not too practical, though."

"You didn't say you wanted something practical," Mark returned mildly. "Do you?"

"I'd rather bend your brain on it than mine," Kyle admitted. "Is anybody still looking for that lost village, or did they find it?"

"Lost—?" Mark moved on into the room and took a seat. "You mean that search a couple of years ago? There was nothing to go on but some vague tradition about a clan that disappeared toward the mountains. No trace was found, so the search was dropped."

Janna's voice was barely audible. "We found . . . something. Maybe a village."

Only Mark's suddenly arrested motion betrayed his interest. He laid the book slowly on a glass-topped end table and stood silent for a long moment before asking, "Where?"

"The lake on old Kelvin's place," Kyle said.

"I've never been out there. It's hard to believe

127

that's it with all the searching that's been done. On the other hand I'd go right now to check it out, if I could." Mark's expression was rueful. "Unfortunately, the school expects some work out of me this afternoon. What have you found exactly?"

"It was Karen, my little sister," Janna said. It wasn't as difficult as she had feared, telling Mark about the lake, though she found herself leaving out the voices, the shadows. He had to know, and still she couldn't tell him. He listened intently through her physical description of the lake, then eased back against the wall, looking thoughtful. "Sounds good, as far as you've gone. Now, what does all that have to do with this?" He hefted the book.

"I think that something happened there, that someone, maybe a lot of people, died." Janna met his eyes for the first time since she'd started. His look was steady and encouraging, and she felt his belief. "I think they're still there."

"Go over it again, from the beginning. Tell me all the parts you've left out" was all he said. Neither Kyle nor Mark interrupted as Janna told the whole story this time, and there was a small silence when she was done. Then Mark leaned forward, chin on one hand.

"What about you, Kyle? Have you seen or heard anything yourself?"

"Nothing you could put your finger on." He frowned. "The place is different somehow, sort of stirred up. I don't know, maybe it feels wrong."

"Good enough." Mark glanced at the clock, then settled more comfortably. "Say there's something there, ghosts possibly. What makes you different, Janna, you and your sister? What makes you susceptible? There's always a reason, something that pulls it all together. What would bind you and Karen to whatever is at the lake?"

"Grief," she said. "Death. There was an accident last winter, and Karen was the only survivor. She thinks she killed Mom."

"That would account for it," Mark said with an honest sympathy. "And your father?"

Kyle broke in. "If he's not an alcoholic yet, he will be soon."

Mark's voice was gentle. "Your family needs counseling, Janna. I'll help you all I can, but this part is beyond me."

"Do we counsel away the ghosts too, Mark? You can be sure they won't make an appointment." Kyle snorted angrily. "What's to stop Karen just disappearing in the meantime?"

"Put a lid on it, Kyle." Mark's tone was friendly. "If there are ghosts, they'll have to be handled separately. And frankly, I don't see any other interpretation. There could be what experts on the paranormal call a psychic imprint. Sometimes, when there is a catastrophe, people's minds react with such shock and horror that it leaves an actual impression,

129

like those plaster handprints you make in kindergarten. That's the theory anyway. Maybe you and Karen can sense that imprint."

"What can we do?" Janna asked.

"Well, quit looking at me so hopefully, both of you. I'm only an amateur. Let me think." Mark moved around the room, his fingertips brushing a book here, an object there. He ended up at last in front of the fireplace. Just as Janna had, he reached out and touched the apron fringe into clattering life. He spoke without turning. "You say you heard something like the dancing rattles?"

"Several times," Janna said.

Mark nudged the deer hooves once more, then turned his back on their fading whisper. "That would be the shaman. If there were a sudden catastrophe, if a whole village died together . . . "

"I heard voices, Mark, last night in the rain. They said they would be salmon spirits. Could that mean they drowned?"

"Probably." Mark went to a shelf, pulled out another book. He stood frowning down at it, turning it over in his hands. "Some Northwest Indian groups believed that the drowned would go to the village of the salmon people, to be born again as salmon and live and die to feed their people. But it's a perilous journey across a bridge in the fog, over a fearful chasm of nothingness. The dead had to be guided by someone living, someone who could sing the songs and call the names and prevent a misstep that would leave them between the worlds forever. Usually that would be a shaman in trance."

Kyle said slowly, "But the shaman—"

"Probably died with the rest," Mark ended. "He could cross himself, but he wouldn't be able to guide the others. There was no one to lead them."

Janna's voice was hoarse, as though she hadn't used it for years. "And my sister?"

He spread his hands. "They might think she could guide them," Mark said simply.

Janna felt all the horror she had denied closing in on her. Kyle's voice seemed dim for a long heartbeat, but it steadied her.

"Karen's not a shaman," he said sharply.

"No, but she's all they've got. Maybe there's some form of communication through their grief." Mark crossed the room and sat down next to Janna. "If what you said about the last moon means what I think it might, then they're out of time. The way stays open only so long as there are enough of their physical remains to hold them in the place of death. When's the dark of the moon?"

Kyle was already checking a calendar in the hall. "Saturday."

"Two more days then," Mark commented. "They're desperate. That's why they're trying Karen. She's probably the first person they've really been able to reach."

"She can't help them," Janna said. Mark hesitated, and she repeated, "She can't."

131

"Children see so clearly, more so than adults." The teacher shifted uncomfortably, looking down at his hands. Plainly, he didn't want to tell her this part. "There are tales of children making their way between the worlds alone and even acting as guides at the moment of death. Any children who drowned with the village would be held by the adults, waiting. But Karen . . . Karen might make it. They'll send her before them."

"No." Janna could tell she was pale. She felt bloodless to the tips of her fingers.

"When you heard the owl speak her name, Karen was marked for death. There's only one way we can change that." He got up and paced back to the coffee table, placing the book carefully atop the other. "We'll have to break the haunting."

He said it so casually that for a long moment it seemed a perfectly natural thing to say, a suggestion well within reason. And then the enormity of it loomed forward, and they could only stare.

Kyle regained his voice first. "Right, we do it every day. *How*, Mark?"

The teacher smiled slightly. "Maybe not us, precisely. I know a present-day shaman. He helped with the search for the lost village. The right people should be able to do something." He consulted his watch. "I have just enough time to make a couple of calls before I go back to school. And you have just enough time to make your next classes, if you run."

132

He scooted them toward the door. Kyle went out ahead of her, and Janna stopped to look back at Mark.

Mark hesitated. "Try not to hate them, Janna."

"I don't," she said truthfully. She wanted to, and she couldn't. "I don't hate them. I'm afraid of them."

14

JANNA WAS HALFWAY HOME THAT afternoon, sitting alone on the bus, when the first raindrops spattered against the grimy windows and started uneasy ripples in her mind. Kyle had gone home with Mark, and she couldn't stop herself from worrying about Karen. Janna could only hope her trust in her father for once would be justified.

The light drizzle stroked her face like cold feathers as the bus faded into the gray distance, and Janna stood hesitating by the side of the road. Safety lay in turning her back on the trail and taking the rutted lane home. But her memories of the lake were a dull, aching burden, pulling and pushing her. She could close herself away in the house, but she couldn't shut them out of her mind. Sighing, she crossed the trickle of water in the ditch and stepped into the trees. She thought the woods, dark and uneasy, made a fitting land for ghosts.

When she reached the lake, she could feel the shadows waiting just beyond sight. The steep valley was filled with an evasive whispering, a shifting al-

134

most of time itself. From all around her, they plucked at her mind, a low murmur of unsound slurring the air, and the white owl drifted from tree to tree. Unreality seemed a part of the very fabric of the world.

The water lay flat under the touch of the rain, a suffocating weight pressing down over the drowned village. Isolation wrapped the standing totems, wrenched from their meaning in the past.

Janna touched the carved surface of Karen's downed totem for the first time. What she felt here wasn't evil. The desperation of fear, a powerful eclipsing misery, yes, but not evil intent. Here there was a bridge to the past. That was what bound Karen so tightly to this place. Her own moment of disaster had never ended, but went on and on, relived in nightmare and reinforced by silence. And the shadow host that waited here whispered and promised, offering perhaps to take a suffering child with them to a place where pain would die.

Her hand dropped away from the softened wood.

"She can't help you," Janna whispered.

She will lead us, she will lead us. There is no other way. . . . It was the barest thread of thought, words twining out of the empty sky into her mind. *The last moon dies, there is no other way.*

Close beside her, Janna felt a stronger presence. Dim and indistinct, a figure wavered at the edge of vision. Weak with the hunger for life, he reached out, deer hoof rattles chattering. Seen and not seen,

135

the figure stood for a long-held breath, and then he was turning away. Turning, turning, and gone. The carved face in front of her stared sightlessly upward, grimacing at the weeping sky, and the voices dissolved in the air. Silenced, they waited. Their pain was everywhere, rising out of the ground and the water like a rampant, choking growth. And deep within, her own pain opened outward like a dark, hungry flower, and suddenly she could stand it no longer.

"You lied! My mother isn't there, she didn't drown!" Janna screamed. A deafening quiet beat back at her, almost a presence in itself. "You lied to Karen! She can't lead you anywhere!"

Her sister's name seemed to linger, a murmur passing from throat to throat, and that was all. Hands clenched, she moved toward the water. Her nails were cutting into her palms, the healing slash on her hand tight and aching.

"Isn't there another way? Tell *me*," she said urgently, pleading. Still the silence, and Janna's voice rose again, breaking. "I won't let her *die!*"

There was no response. Then through the gray misting rain a sliver of sound shifted on the breeze, touching world to world. Out of nowhere, out of nothing, Janna heard the desolate crying of a child. For a frozen moment there was only that single voice, weaving among the trees, then another began, and another. All around her unseen children wailed,

136

drifting toward the lake, out over the water, until at last the cold silence took them.

There was no other answer.

Eyes wide with horror, Janna backed away from the water, spun on her heel, and ran.

Janna paused outside the house to catch her breath. She stopped running only when she burst through the last whipping branches and skidded in the mud at the edge of the lane, bringing her abruptly to a sense of the present. Her own ragged breathing replaced the echoes of crying in her ears.

Calmer now, Janna opened the door. Karen, dressed in her nightgown, lay sprawled asleep on the floor beside her father's chair. Half smiling, Dad looked up from the old Japanese movie that flickered on the TV screen.

"You come to save me from this movie? I'm afraid Karen will wake up if I turn it off," he complained amiably.

"How is she?" Janna hung up her coat and ran an exploratory hand through her hair. It was tangled and damp.

"Pretty good. She's still a little cool, and she didn't want much to eat. I had to threaten to sit on her to keep her in, though. She wanted to go to the lake."

"What did she say?" Janna asked sharply.

"Nothing much. Come off it, Janna. It's no big deal. All kids imagine things."

"It's real, Dad."

He wasn't listening anymore. He stretched in the chair, stifling a yawn. "I don't know if I could handle much more of this. Think I'll go out tonight."

"I wish you wouldn't, Dad." It was hard to keep her voice steady. "Please?"

He looked at her doubtfully. "We'll see. By the way, have you been messing with those bottles again?"

Her hesitation was almost imperceptible. "No," she lied.

"Hmph. Could've sworn I bought more than that." He settled himself more comfortably, his attention going back to the screen now that the movie was over. He said casually over his shoulder, "Kyle called. Said he'd be over in a little while. You two got plans for tonight?"

"Homework, I guess."

"I like him." Her dad sounded surprised. "Never thought I'd care for any guy that started hanging around one of my daughters, but he's all right."

"Yeah, he's all right." She leaned over the top of the chair suddenly and kissed her father's forehead. His green eyes met hers upside down, and he smiled, the old closeness bridging the gap between them. And then the moment was gone. His eyes edged away from hers, from the potential for hurt, and returned to the TV. In a separate unreality, the people on the screen simpered back vacuously. Janna left them together and went upstairs for dry clothes.

Dad was in his room when she came down again. She bent over Karen, feeling the coolness of her skin, smothering a pang of worry. Her sister stirred, eyelids flickering, and sank into sleep once more. Janna covered her gently with an afghan and went on into the kitchen.

A beer can, still beaded with sweat, lay empty in the sink. This was Dad's idea of taking it easy on the booze. She crumpled it in disgust and dropped it in the garbage. There were more, squat and full, lurking in the fridge. And somewhere her dad had found a bottle with a last measure of whiskey in it. It stood on the counter, waiting. She was tempted to dump it, but knew she could never get away with that. It would have been a useless gesture anyway.

A light knock fell on the front door. Janna hurried to open it, hoping the sound hadn't wakened Karen.

"Hi." Kyle stepped inside and gestured casually at the figure by his side. Behind them the rain was falling harder, a gray curtain. "Mark invited himself over."

He was grinning, but the other man looked unusually somber as he followed him in. Kyle's grin faded when he saw Karen curled up on the floor. Janna led them back into the kitchen.

"She feeling better?" Kyle asked.

"I think so. She's been asleep ever since I got home."

"Best thing for her." Mark took off his windbreaker, dark with wet, and hung it over the back of the nearest chair. "From the little I saw just now, I'd say you've probably found the village all right. The crests Karen's uncovered on the totem support the idea pretty strongly." Grasping the chair, he leaned forward. "I'm not a strong sensitive, Janna, but I tried to feel if there was anything there. The impressions I got were vague, mostly cold water, darkness, and overwhelming grief, but it was enough to make me think we're on the right track. It's a place of the dead."

Kyle moved a restless pace. "So where does that bring us, Mark?" Janna sensed that it wasn't the first time in the last hour that he had asked that question. Mark shrugged.

"It gives us someplace to start. The tribes will be interested in the site, and the museum preservation society as well. They've both been looking for this one for some time." Mark straightened, releasing the chair. "Aside from the burial ceremonies, they'll want to secure the artifacts there, especially that fallen totem. It's in a remarkable state, considering its age. And the crest poles are just the beginning, you know."

"They'll take them away?" Janna asked hoarsely. Those others would have nothing then, she thought, no anchor against the darkness. "How will that help?"

"Everything they ever cared about is there, Janna. Even their bodies are lying unburied in the woods and under the water. Afraid to go on, they've clung to those fragments of their lives." He shrugged again. "Those things have been their salvation and their prison for over a hundred years. It's time we set them free."

"Free to do what, Mark?" Kyle asked. The fading bruise was livid on his face. "To just drift forever?"

"Of course not. I called one of the shamans, Alan Whitewater, this morning just after you left. He'll sing them across, as soon as we line up coordination with the museum. It's going to be difficult to get them to agree to do anything very urgently." Mark glanced at his watch and lifted his jacket. "I'll make some more phone calls tonight to see what I can do in that direction. And now I really need to get going, or I'll be correcting tests until dawn. Coming, Kyle?"

Janna's father appeared in the doorway. "Karen in here?"

"She's sleeping." Something inside Janna went very quiet as her father slowly shook his head. "Isn't she?"

Janna pushed past him into the other room. Kyle and Mark followed her. Karen had been left for such a short time, not even really alone. She had to be still there. Janna's mind refused the sight of the afghan that lay in a crumpled heap in the shadows. Behind her, her father was speaking, his voice ragged with concern.

"I checked your room before I came down. Everything's just like it was when she got up to watch TV

141

hours ago. She's not upstairs, or in the bathroom, and she's not here, so I thought she'd be in the kitchen with you."

"She'll have gone to the lake," Kyle said grimly.

Mark was already sliding into his jacket. "Then let's go."

Kyle's voice, Mark's, were a slow garble in her ears, a meaningless sound track running down. Janna took it all in from a distance, divorced from the reality of it. In her mind she heard again the sound of crying, ripping her heart. Her sister was gone.

Strong hands gripped her shoulders, and Mark's voice fell bracingly on her ears. "Janna, snap up. Come on." She tore her gaze from the incongruous brightness of the tumbled afghan.

"We have to go after her," she said numbly.

"We will, as fast as we can scramble. I just wanted to be sure you were here with us on planet Earth," Mark said, steering her toward the door.

Dad had already gone, shouldering past her and running for the path. They ran after him through the wet dregs of the afternoon, and the cold Janna felt was the icy touch of still water, closing around her sister. It was a long, bitter trail to the lake.

They burst into the clearing one by one, sliding to a halt. Janna's gaze flew first to the fallen totem. The wind rushed briefly through the high trees, the rain needled her skin, and all she knew was that Karen wasn't there. They were too late. From inside

142

her, the world began to collapse. Then Kyle turned her gently and pointed.

"There."

"I see her," Dad answered. And Janna froze.

The scene seemed to magnify, the vastness of the trees expanding to fill the world, the ridges shouldering aside the sky. The crumbling wooden corpses of long-dead trees appeared wavery and twisted, unimportant. Like Janna, dwindling into themselves.

It was the totem poles that commanded the scene, stark gray against the deep green of the far shore. They had dropped their cloaking anonymity at last under the darkening sky. And at the base of the tallest, fingers entwined in the heavy moss, was Karen.

In the closing daylight her nightgown was a smudge of weak pink. She might have been painted on the dark background, she stood so still. If she heard them, she gave no sign of it. There was a greater distance separating them, somehow, than the few feet of shallow water. Karen had become a part of the future-past of this place.

They stood stiff and dumb, the four of them like grim-faced mannequins. Janna knew her own face must look carved from granite, but her father's was the worst. His was contorted with the strain of having to come face-to-face in a moment with all the things he had tried so hard to deny and bury. His shell was cracking at last, and with it all the protection he had. Janna couldn't bear any more and looked away.

Above her sister's head, the owl perched unmoving, ghostly white. The yellow eyes were fixed on Karen in an unblinking stare, until they shifted to Janna. Meeting that flat, alien gaze, she at last understood.

They were all caught now in the moment that had never ended. And when it finally did—here, now—Karen was to go with it. Past and future converged and spun together, spiraling toward this single breath of eternity. This was the last singing of the song, the final calling.

Her father was the first to break the immobility that held them all. His gaze riveted on Karen as though she were the only thing in life, he moved slowly forward. His soaked shirt clung to shoulders that had lost some of their power in his months of despair, but he seemed straighter and stronger now than at any other time in the last harrowing months. Janna doubted if he felt the water lapping around his ankles when he stopped.

"Oh, lord," he breathed.

15

HER FATHER STOOD STONE STILL IN THE water. Night was seeping from under the trees, the shadows flowing outward, full of flickering insubstantial faces that disappeared under Janna's gaze. The air was tense with an expectant silence.

"Karen." Her father spoke softly, afraid of startling her. There was no response. "Baby, come on now. I'm here to take you home."

The silence drew out, until Janna thought there would be no answer. Then at last Karen's voice drifted over the water.

"I promised, Daddy." Her voice broke, and she went on. "I have to go."

"Come here to me, and we'll talk about it." Under cover of his words, her dad moved a cautious stride forward. The water crept up his calves. Janna and Kyle stood silent, hardly daring to breathe for fear of shattering the tenuous contact. His next words seemed wrung out of him, as though he tried to hold them back. "Not you, too, baby, please. Don't go."

Mark started wading quietly into the deepening

dusk, shrugging out of his jacket and throwing it back to the beach. "Keep trying."

The low voice barely reached Janna, but it seemed to steady her father. His deep breath and answering nod were hardly perceptible. "Come on, sweetheart."

"I can't, Daddy. Mamma's waiting, they promised." Karen tipped her head, listening into the hush, and a sob caught in her throat. "I want to tell her I'm sorry."

"No." That single word was a painful moan. "It wasn't you, baby. It wasn't you."

But Karen stood as motionless as the totems. Only her nightgown moved, tugged by the invisible fingers of the currents around her knees. The air around them pulsed with the voices of singers long dead; Karen's voice at first was no more than a thread woven into the rain. She missed a word, hesitating, then caught the rhythm with a new strength. The two melodies braided together, blending.

Head thrown back, Karen sang down the night.

The sound slashed through Janna. The shadows had taught Karen the words, the keys to turn as she walked out into the water, and the drowned would lead the drowned. If there was a gateway here to the past, or the future, or something not quite either, it opened only one way. There was only one direction to time. Did Karen understand that? With a deep, stabbing pain, Janna thought perhaps she did.

146

She thought Karen would welcome the silence and the clear darkness.

Kyle touched her shoulder as they moved toward the lake, following Mark and her father. "It can't stay shallow for much farther. She's probably at the edge of the drop-off."

Janna nodded and walked out into the water. The shock of its touch ran through her like a current. The lake was theirs, more truly than ever before. Its silken caress sang through her body with an intensity that shivered within her bones. Janna faltered, and ahead of her Mark stopped, head tilted as though listening to some other voice. Then Kyle reached him, and they went on together. They grew indistinct, moving away from her into the dusk.

Janna struggled to keep moving, but the music was a wall this time, holding her prisoned and half-tranced. Through the water, she could feel the fierce agony of the shadows' longing, invading her, throbbing in her veins. Nothing else mattered beside it.

Janna slowed and finally stopped, unable to go on.

The others were mere shadows in the failing light. Only Karen had any real substance, glowing in pale color against the somber dregs of the day. Beyond her the lost ones waited, a clot of darker darkness along the shore, their wanting heavy and real as hunger. Janna forced herself to breathe against that heartbeat of ancient sorrow. It was useless trying to shut her mind against the sense of transparent past

147

overlaying the present, but she refused to let it swallow her.

Karen's voice rose in volume, clear and commanding, and stopped abruptly on a final note. The sound of a shaken rattle echoed through the clearing.

The owl moved then, shifting atop the totem pole, settling feathers beaded with rain. It threw back its head, face to the sky, and from its throat came the sounds Janna had been dreading. The names. The owl called, and Karen echoed that slow chant like swelling waves. The shadows would be named, and it would be done. Karen would die.

And there was nothing Janna could do, not even follow.

She could stand no more. A scream rose through the layers of paralyzing fear within her like a bubble through cloudy liquid.

"Stop lying to her!" she cried. The owl swiveled its head, the yellow eyes stabbing at her, and the voices paused. The world came back into normal focus, and she could be aware again of her father, of Kyle and Mark moving slowly forward. Karen, tense, half turned her head. Seeing that, Janna went on, more quietly. "She isn't there, Karen. Mom didn't drown."

A shudder seemed to shake her sister's shoulders. Karen's head dropped, and across the darkening water a despairing whisper reached Janna. "She has to be there."

148

The others were close, almost close enough, when Karen raised her head and with the owl called out the final names. Her father stretched to reach her, but she was just beyond his fingertips. Without looking around, Karen stepped away, and the water deepened around her. Another yard, and she stopped. The voices whispered thinly, urging her forward. Only one step remained.

Karen teetered there a long moment, hesitating on the edge of life. Janna struggled against the power that held her, desperate to reach her sister. She managed two dragging steps forward, and that was all. Far beyond her, Kyle reached outward, fingers stretching to touch Karen's arm. And she was gone, the water closing soundlessly over her head.

Mark and Kyle dove from where they stood, a second behind Janna's father. The disturbance set the water lapping against the totems, around Janna's legs, and against the bottomless silence of the waiting shadows. The agony of watching seemed endless, as some part of Janna's mind ticked off the seconds. The coming night pressed down, and she could only vaguely see the shape that broke the surface at long last, as a voice choked out, "Here!"

The three dove under the water once more. The surface thrashed as they kicked themselves down, and then grew ominously quiet. The fear that none of them would ever come up sprouted in Janna's mind, as time spun out unnaturally. The stillness was broken twice in a strange syncopated rhythm as the men came up to gulp a few ragged breaths, and disappear once more. Janna felt a wordless, formless prayer taking shape in her heart. Karen had been down too long.

The lake's surface was healing itself, smoothing into an unbroken sheet that denied the struggle below. And then, one by one, Janna heard more than saw them break through. Angry ripples fled in pale circles across the dark water. An indistinguishable murmur carried to her ears, and then one figure stood out of the water. She couldn't make out who it was. He turned back, stooped, and something was passed up to him, and he waded toward shore. The others pulled themselves out of the water behind him.

Out of the twilight, her father came, with Karen in his arms. She was pale and still, one limp hand swaying in time with his movement. His face was haggard and set in lines of renewed grief. Janna closed her eyes briefly against the sight, and the expectant silence of those others beat against her. They still waited, willing Karen to go on before them. It wasn't over yet, then. A fragile thread of life held Karen to the world.

Janna felt Mark jostle past her, rushing to shore. "Is she breathing?"

Her father shook his head in numb silence, laying his daughter on the ground. Nightgown torn and muddied, hair tangled and heavy with water, Karen lay with frightening stillness.

Mark stepped across her bare legs, kneeling next to her and pressing an ear to her chest. "On her side, quick."

A few drops of water trickled from Karen's mouth as she was pushed urgently onto her side, nothing more. Janna felt a spark of dark victory jump among the lost ones. Karen's hold on life was loosening. Their voices were a deep thrumming, *"She will lead us, she will lead us!"*

Mark tilted Karen's head back to open an airway, muttering, "Come on, come on," and he started to ease her back to begin rescue breathing. Karen's arms and legs jerked suddenly, and then a retching spasm shook the small body. Water gushed from her mouth, and Karen took a sobbing, coughing breath. It caught in her throat, hesitated, and Janna felt another surge of hope from those others. Karen's chest heaved, and finally her breathing fell into a regular rhythm. And silently, an invisible door inched nearly shut, and Janna's feet were freed. She staggered forward as the shadows streamed past, keening a painful cry that dissolved against the icy bondage of the lake.

Janna touched her sister's face as their father gathered Karen awkwardly into his arms and clung to her fiercely. A deep gash on his forearm bled a weak orange stain into the soaked fabric of Karen's nightgown. He seemed not to feel it. Kyle came to put a protective arm around Janna as her father pushed himself unsteadily to his feet.

Mark picked up Kyle's wool jacket from the ground where it had been thrown, and placed it around Karen. Her father nodded again. "I'd better get her to the hospital."

"You'll need help driving," Mark said.

Kyle ran a hand through his plastered hair, flipping it out of his eyes with a weary toss. "I'll go along."

They turned away and in a few steps were swallowed by the trees. Janna wanted to go with them, but felt a curious reluctance to leave the haunted clearing. Mark had wandered away to stand staring down at the exposed face of the fallen totem, reaching out to touch it thoughtfully with his toe.

It was his voice that finally broke the silence.

" 'The white man will never be alone,' he said." Mark spoke over his shoulder, still nudging the carving. "He said, 'When the memory of my tribe shall have become a myth among the white man, these shores will swarm with the invisible dead of my tribe.' Appropriate, don't you think?"

"Who said it, Mark?" Janna tried to control her shivering, without much success.

"Chief Sealth—Seattle, they call him now. The day they forced him to sign over the whole Northwest coast and half the salmon, forever." His foot dropped from the wood, and he turned toward her once more. "You're freezing. I'd better walk you home, then I'll go call Whitewater again. The sooner this is ended, the better."

152

Janna nodded miserably. "I remember what you said, about not hating them. I feel like I should, Mark, for trying to take Karen. And I can't," she said, looking out over the water. She thought about the bitter weeks after her mother's death, how she had wanted to hate the driver who had shattered her life. But he had paid the ultimate price, blood for blood, life for life. Like those others here. "I can't hate them, I can't hate the man who killed my mother—what's wrong with me?"

His voice was gentle behind her. "Nothing, Janna. You have the strength to let go, that's all, and the compassion to understand their pain. Don't turn away from the gift."

And remembering the ache of longing in those other hearts, in her own, she sighed. "It would be easier to hate."

"It's always easier to hate." His face was a pale blur in the falling night, his hand a separate blur as he moved past her and beckoned her forward. Janna turned toward home, but made no other move to follow him.

"Will Karen be all right?"

Mark hesitated, and in the near darkness Janna could just make out the movement of his shoulders. "I'd like to say yes, Janna, but I just don't know. Karen was down a long time. I think she'll live, but beyond that . . . "

"It may have been for nothing, then." Janna heard the whisper come out of the deep hollow inside her, felt the despair crowding behind it. "She may be just like them, now, caught between . . . "

"We can't know yet, Janna. All we can do is wait."

Mark took her arm, and, muscles tight with chill, she went with him, home to begin the waiting.

16

JANNA FELT A HAND LAID SOFTLY ON the back of her head and started. She hadn't meant to fall asleep, hunched over the kitchen table. The muscles in her neck burned in protest as she turned her head. "Dad," she muttered, and straightened groggily. "How's Karen?"

"No brain damage," he said, pouring a cup of the waiting coffee and dropping into a chair at the table, staring moodily into the mug. He was wearing baggy hospital greens instead of his own wet clothing. "They said it's too early yet to be sure about pneumonia, and she's suffering from hypothermia, but it looks pretty good."

"Can I see her, Dad?"

He shook his head. "Not tonight. They've put her under pretty heavily anyway. She was thrashing around and crying."

There seemed nothing to say to that, and a silence dropped between them. Karen would be all right. Janna felt weak with relief, but her father was tense. He raised his coffee, and put it down untasted. At

155

last he muttered something under his breath and stood up, rattling his chair and bumping the table. The nearly empty bottle still stood on the counter. He pulled a glass from the cupboard and jerked the whiskey to him. Janna bit back a comment as the last of the liquid splashed into the glass.

He leaned back against the counter and stared for a long minute down into the glass, swirling it in small careful circles. And then he turned slowly, not looking at Janna, and deliberately poured his drink down the drain. With his back still to her, he put the glass down with a click in the sink and spoke to the wall above it.

"It hasn't helped anything, has it?"

"No, Dad. It's just taken you away from us as well."

"Karen still believes she was responsible." He seemed to be forcing the words out, still facing away from her. "I should have seen, should have done something. Instead I put it all onto you."

"I know." Janna's voice was little more than a whisper. The clock ticked loudly as her father stood with his back to the room, and there was nothing she could say to fill the silence.

"There's got to be some way to make it work," he said then, turning.

Janna traced a design on the table where her own cup had left a ring earlier. "It won't be easy after all this time."

"It never was. I tried the easy way, and look where

156

it's gotten me. I'm halfway to becoming a sodden bum, and my daughters—oh, lord." He broke off, running his hands down over his eyes. He looked sick, and the shivers he had held off suddenly began to shake him. "It was a death trap down there, Janna, branches everywhere. She wasn't fighting, just looked at me with her eyes wide. So calm, like she was dead already. I was afraid we'd never get her up."

Janna started to speak, then changed her mind. Somehow she knew they would never talk about the ghosts. Whatever he had seen, whatever he had heard, it would be rationalized into a shape he could handle. "She thinks you blame her, Dad."

He shook his head, and the tension slowly left his body. "I never did. I was just glad she was all right." He lifted his head, trying to catch her gaze. "I'm sorry, Janna. I've made a fine mess of it."

"It's not too late, not yet." Janna let her eyes meet his at last and saw the same image that haunted her own. "Talk to her about Mom."

"I'll try. It still hurts, as much as it ever did." One corner of his mouth pulled into a wry half smile. "Probably preserved in alcohol."

There was another silence, heaving with the ticking clock and the restless night outside. Her father stared thoughtfully at the bare wall.

"Marta," he said at last, hesitating. After a pause he went on, voice low. "I couldn't even say her name, it hurt so much. I think I wanted to die, too.

Can you understand that, Janna? I loved her so much."

"I know," Janna repeated, through a tight throat. "We did too."

He stood away from the counter then and rested one hand lightly on her hair. "I'm sorry, JJ. I'll talk to the doctor when I get back to the hospital, see if he can tell me what to do. I don't think I remember how to face a day on my own anymore."

"Can you do it?" She hadn't meant to say that, but he didn't flinch.

"I have to, Janna. It'll be a long haul, I'm afraid, but I'll learn." He lifted his hand from her head to check his watch. "Right now I've got to change and get back to your sister. I should be there when she wakes up from sedation. Will you be all right here?"

"Yes." Janna stayed where she was, limp in her chair, as he left. Maybe, just maybe, it would come out all right after all.

They came for the village on Saturday.

In the gray early morning, before she thought anyone would be there, Janna walked to the lake. She had been to see her sister the night before, and the memory made a suffocating weight in her chest. Karen was awake, but so distant it was like she'd gone beyond life, out of the world.

Janna stepped out of the woods and came face-to-face with a tall man in faded denims. His short black hair was shot with silver, his dark face weathered

158

by sun and wind. The deep eyes that met Janna's held a stillness like she had never encountered before, with currents of humor and understanding. He measured her a long moment before he spoke.

"After all you have suffered here, yet you come. Why?" he asked quietly.

She hadn't thought about it, hadn't tried to give a reason to her feeling that she had to be here. Janna touched the faded images in her mind and tried to put words to her thoughts. "I came for them. To see it have a final ending at last."

"A final ending, or a proper beginning. Who can say?" He looked away across the lake. "I'm Alan Whitewater. I, too, come for them."

His voice had brought a troubling into the sadness of this place, a thread of recognition in the air. Faintly, Janna thought she heard the voices whisper, *Grandson.* Startled, she looked at him. He nodded. He had heard it too.

"I am honored to be named grandson by such as these. I will do my best to honor them in return." His fathomless eyes followed a flutter of white, watched as the owl came to perch on a branch above Karen's totem. "So, the Guardian remains. There can be no evil here."

"I know," Janna answered softly. A gust of wind pushed past her and ruffled the still surface, spinning an eddy of hopeless despair into the air. "And yet my sister nearly died."

"Your sister nearly died," he agreed solemnly.

159

The deep eyes met Janna's again. "They must have waited many dark years, and no one came. Only your troubled little Karen, who could hear the songs and feel the pain. They could not know if another would ever come."

"Mark said they were out of time. How can that be?"

"They know, as your people do not, that any part of a thing contains the essence of the whole. As long as they could not cross to the salmon village they would be held here by the things they valued in life. Now time has rotted away the bonds that hold them against the dark, and soon they would be adrift in the nothing between the worlds, if it weren't for your sister."

What he said was true. It was through Karen this man had finally come. Through her the forgotten were found. She had truly been their last hope, yet Janna felt a shadow of bitterness. "My mother isn't there with them. She can't be. They lied."

"Have you never wished to believe what could not be?"

The quiet question stopped her. In the silence a distant chain saw sputtered into life. Another joined it, and another, until they were a chorus of metal demons gnawing a narrow slash through the woods. Finally Janna nodded, shoving her hands deep into her pockets.

"They will dance tonight by the ghost fires of the salmon people, and they would have given Karen the same afterlife they wished for themselves." He started to move toward the fallen totem. "I will set them free, but there is nothing more I can do for your sister. That will be up to you and your father, and it may be the hardest of all."

Janna followed him across the muddy beach. "They can't get her to talk or eat. She won't even look at us, just turns her face to the wall."

"She still hears them calling. Karen will be better when they call no more. Then the healing can begin."

Whitewater squatted beside the leering wooden face, tracing its worn carvings with a gentle, almost loving hand. He spoke more to the downed giant than to her, his voice tinged with regret. "My father once did work such as this. I went to university to become a white man and learned too late what it meant to be truly Indian. My father was gone then, and his skills with him." The hands stopped their wanderings. "There is something here, something more than the rest."

Dark fingers, sensitive and long, removed a strip of moss. "The wood is better preserved than I expected. The ones below are protected by some chemistry of the water, but this one should be more like those"—he jerked his head toward the standing poles—"with the faces eaten away by time."

The demon sounds of the saws had drawn closer, and looking over her shoulder Janna could just see a Jeep, groping its way toward the clearing. Its angry

161

whine beat against the quiet, out of place and time. Workers with saws moved ahead of it, others rode or walked behind.

Kyle and Mark dropped from the moving Jeep as it entered the clearing. At a gesture from White-water, the engine was shut off, and silence descended again. Even the creaking of branches and rustling of leaves were subdued.

Kyle came to stand beside her, and together they watched tools and diving equipment unloaded from the truck. A heavy tarp was spread in front of Karen's totem pole, and the brush and moss carefully cleared from its surface. Mark came over to stand on Janna's other side as padded cables were looped around it.

"I'm afraid they'll have to give this one to the museum," he said, gesturing toward the totem leering at the sky with face upon lifeless face.

"Why?" Kyle asked curiously.

"Half the money for this project was theirs." Mark's smile held little amusement. "We had to bargain away the best of the totems in order to keep all the remains for burial."

"How will they find the bodies?" Janna asked. After all this time the earth would have hidden them well, she thought. Mark seemed unconcerned.

"Whitewater has his ways. They'll all be found." His attention had gone beyond her. "Look, they're ready."

The Jeep's engine coughed into life once more,

and the winch groaned as it drew the cables taut. Janna felt the sudden tension, thought she could almost hear the dark chanting once more, weary and fragile as the rotting wood. Or maybe it was only the wind. Men stood on the canvas ready to ease the log over as it came, others pushed at it from behind. There was a tearing sound as the totem began to roll, tipping so that the familiar face stared across the clearing.

The moment stretched, as the great crest pole hesitated, heavy underside hanging suspended over its damp bed. The earth seemed reluctant to let go its claim. Then the final invasive roots tore free, and the totem rolled with a thump onto the canvas, the carved features hidden once again.

A murmur of sound broke from the men nearest the pole, and they surged forward, but Whitewater motioned them back even as he knelt. His eyes caught hers, and Janna shoved through the circle of workers, obeying the summons in his look.

She pushed aside the last protesting worker and stopped. Standing alone beside the older man, she felt another presence, the smoky shadow of a shape, and a face that this time didn't turn away.

The underside of the log before her was dark with age and decay, returning to the earth that had harbored its life and embraced its death. Large chunks of rotting wood remained in the pressed bed, exposing the drier, brighter wood near the totem's heart. A sifting of debris slid from its sides and

163

pattered onto the tarp, loud in the silence. Some of the men backed away.

Gently, Whitewater brushed aside crumbling bits of wood on the ground in front of him and touched a scatter of fragmented bone. "Find rest, Grandfather."

A flutter of motion overhead, and the white owl launched itself and dropped to earth beside the shattered skull. Hunching its body, it spread stealthy hunter's wings above the crushed eye sockets. Strange golden eyes met Janna's, then shifted to Whitewater's, as time spun together into a single strand of future-past.

After an endless moment, the bird warbled a plaintive note, crouching even lower, and Janna thought it would take off. Then there was a sigh in the air, and a nod of finality from the figure who stood beyond the edge of the world. Over bones grown porous and brittle with time, the owl began to cry.

The Indians stood with faces impassive, the museum workers uncomfortable but silent. Janna wondered how many felt the unseen others pressing forward. On and on the strange, haunting voice called, never repeating. The names rolled into the stillness, fifty-seven, and Whitewater's eyes never left the Guardian. The flame of memory passed on.

In another world a rattle was shaken, and out of the air a voice spoke, directly into her mind. A single, final phrase, and then silence.

"You have done well," Whitewater murmured,

reaching forward. "I will guard your trust."

His fingertips brushed the owl, and for a moment it stared up at him, golden eyes dimming. Then their light went out, and its body seemed to lose its shape. Protecting wings wavered, sinking, feathers stretching out as in flight. As Janna watched, the night bird slowly began to collapse, falling inward, dissolving against the ground. The dark earth drank its substance, until there was nothing left but a handful of crumpled feathers scattering on the breeze. They swirled together and came to rest inside a broken circle of deer hooves.

The waiting was done.

EPILOGUE

It was over.

An infant night layered over the narrow valley, and the rain slithered and pattered on the branches and the darkening water. In the shadows where the great pole had lain, a figure waited, listening. He heard nothing but the sounds of water striking water and living things growing toward the sky. The lake drank the gift of the clouds without a murmur. The voices were stilled.

The lake, at last, was alone.

The water was cloudy with stirred silt, drifting downward to blur the edges of fresh scars. Deepening night drew muffling shadows over raw earth where men had worked, hid the gaps in the ranks of standing snags. All would shortly be as it should. Strong grandsons had done their work well.

They had gone, those patient waiting ones. The last moon was dying on the horizon, their time was done, and they had gone. All but the last. He-who-walks-between-the-worlds stood as he had for long and long, between life and afterlife, to watch until the final moment.

166

The wind scattered wild patterns across the water and caught at a broken feather on the ground. From the woods floated the cry of a spirit hunter, and the lone one nodded. The Guardian, too, had been freed. It was well.

The silt settled as the night drew down deep, and black, and needled with rain. Beyond the clouds the moon grew darker, and yet he waited. He stood silent, a pool of deeper night, listening. Nothing. The rain was called away over the mountain, and at last the moon died in the sky. It was time. The door was closing, and he must go through. The small one with the hungering grief would not come. The waiting was done.

A vague motion in the blackness, a silent whisper of song, and a swaying sense of clattering deer hoof rattles; there was nothing more to the steps of the final dance. Just a moving darkness, and a pale blur of a face, turning, and gone.